GOTHIC BLUE BOOK V
The Cursed Edition

Edited by
Cynthia (Cina) Pelayo & Gerardo Pelayo

ISBN-10: 098473046X
ISBN-13: 978-0-9847304-6-9

Cover art by Lenka Šimečková - llesim.tumblr.com

CONTENTS

INTRODUCTION

Gothic Blue Books were dark cousins of chapbooks and their popularity peaked between the 1800s and early 1900s. They were abridgements, so shorter versions, of Gothic novels which made them very cheap. These tiny tales of terror were often set in dark castles, cursed abbeys, and haunted houses.

This year's collection is called the Cursed Edition because many of the places featured hold an imprint of something terrible that happened. Many also feature cursed buildings, houses - and people. Some people use the word 'curse' jokingly, but some religions, beliefs and cultures do believe that objects, places, and people can become overwhelmed by misfortune. It's often thought that people can place curses on others, or on objects with the hope that harm and hurt will be inflicted. Whether or not you believe in curses there are those that not only believe in them but believe they can place them – so beware.

In this collection you will find haunted and cursed hotels, an old woman who enjoys to knit quietly – keeping her dark secret guarded. There is a meeting with Robert the Doll – believe created with Voodoo, and of course there is a meeting with our dear friend Death.

We hope that you enjoy this, our fifth Gothic Blue Book – The Cursed Edition featuring fiction by Maria Alexander and poetry Stephanie M. Wytovich.

Cynthia (cina) Pelayo
Gravedigger/Publisher
Burial Day Books

SOME DIVINE
Maria Alexander

Maria Alexander is a produced screenwriter, published games writer, virtual world designer, award-winning copywriter, interactive theatre designer, prolific fiction writer, snarkiologist and poet. Her stories have appeared in publications such as *Chizine Magazine*, *Gothic.net* and *Paradox*, as well as in acclaimed anthologies alongside legends such as David Morrell and Heather Graham.

Her debut novel, *Mr. Wicker*, won the 2014 Bram Stoker Award for Superior Achievement in a First Novel. *Publisher's Weekly* called it, "(a) splendid, bittersweet ode to the ghosts of childhood," while *Library Journal* hailed it in a Starred Review as "a horror novel to anticipate." She's represented by Alex Slater at Trident Media Group.

When she's not wielding a katana at her local shinkendo dojo, she's being outrageously spooky or writing Doctor Who filk. She lives in Los Angeles with two ungrateful cats, a pervasive sense of doom, and a purse called Trog.

First appeared in Songs from Dead Singers…and Other Eulogies from Catalyst Press, edited by Michael Kelly, ©2002

Tears from the depth of some divine despair
Rise in the heart, and gather to the eyes,
In looking on the happy Autumn fields,
And thinking of the days that are no more…

> *"Tears, Idle Tears," by Lord Alfred Tennyson*

Eeep! Eeep!
 The overturned nest rested beneath a sycamore tree in Griffith Park. I

almost stepped on it as I was about to settle down on the grass and read some Yeats. Under the tightly woven womb of twigs and twine I found three small, broken bodies covered with black down. Baby crows. Two of them had died when they struck the ground. The third lived.

I cupped my hands around his quivering body. My heart broke as he turned an inky eye up at me and a pitiful cry escaped his tiny beak. I took him to the car, tucked him into a box of tissue, and drove to the veterinarian near my apartment on Hollywood Boulevard.

The night before, my friend Kevin had given me a tarot reading on my living room rug. He'd turned up a card with a white dove diving straight down from the sky into a silver chalice: The Ace of Cups. He then laid the Death card across it and flashed me a flirty smile. "It looks like you're going to fall in love...and it will transform you."

At least his readings are improving, I thought as the vet tech led us to a small room that smelled of dog hair and antiseptic.

After the veterinarian bandaged the bird's teensy broken leg, he held open the sharp beak with gloved fingers and squirted brown mush from a plastic syringe. "You'll need to hand feed him this mush twice a day, mixing in the medicine. He'll live," he said, "but he'll need the antibiotics for months."

Swallowing bitter visions of credit card bills, I agreed.

That night, the cage sat under a faded black pillowcase on the chest of drawers near my bedroom window. My tiny fuzzball eeped until we both fell asleep.

...Fresh as the first beam glittering on a sail,
That brings our friends up from the underworld...

The next morning, Kevin arrived.

A mutual friend had introduced us about a year earlier at a party for USC Lit grads. Said friend had told me everything about him: his cowboy boots and frock coat, his Scottish band called The Wicker Man, his obsession with H.P. Lovecraft. *An embarrassing geek,* I thought.

But then I saw him: shoulder-length sable brown hair, azure blue eyes, a strong jaw that cradled a *dramatis personae* of witty and compassionate expressions. A grand champion U.S. "slam" team performer with an MFA in Music, Kevin recited Tennyson to the room of once-jaded, now-breathless Literary Criticism majors *(...deep as love/Deep as first love, and wild with all regret...).*

But our mutual friend had purposely failed to tell me that Kevin had a girlfriend that she hated. She'd hoped that Kevin would fall in love with me instead.

I did, too. I fell for him. Hard.

We developed a strong friendship around our mutual passion for poetry and dark aesthetics. I enjoyed his terrible tarot readings and his infectious energy. And as his relationship grew restless, he shared ever more passionate poetry with me. My hopes blossomed. He meant everything to me.

Maybe today would be the day.

I led him into the bedroom and showed him the baby crow. Kevin marveled at the wee black fuzzball, gently stroking the down of his tiny head with one fiddle-callused finger. "Carrine, did you know you've got a psychopomp?"

"No. What's that?"

"Anything that guides the souls of the dead to the underworld. Like the Greek god Hermes. But most birds are, too."

"Hermes," I whispered as I returned the baby crow to the cage. "That's a good name." I carried his cage to the living room and opened the blinds. Bands of sunlight warmed the apartment. "They have the brains of four-year-old children," I explained, trying to impress him with my new birdy lore. "The vet told me he'll learn to speak sentences."

"Really? That's amazing."

"So, where're we going today?"

"Catalina!" he announced. "Passing your oral exams is a big deal. You deserve it."

The Queen Mary's black stacks loomed over us as Kevin's jeep plowed through the parking lot towards the ferry dock next to the giant ship. But by the time we reached the tourist counter, the ferry had already left. The next one wouldn't be departing for three hours.

Disappointed, we wandered back to the parking lot. I leaned against the jeep door, eyeing the mammoth ship. A cruise ship in the 1930s, the Queen Mary was even used in WWII by the U.S. Navy.

"The ship is supposed to be haunted, isn't it?" I asked.

Kevin opened the jeep door to deposit his heavy camera. "That's what they say."

"Then let's go ghost hunting." I pointed to his camera, smiling. "That's how we'll catch them."

Ticket booth elevators deposited us on the lowest ship's deck. The wooden corridors were half-lit by sunlight streaming through rows of tall, narrow windows. We passed expensive dessert shops and ancient kiosks of enlarged old celebrity photos. ("Hello, Bing! Goodbye, Bob!")

"What makes you think this will work?" Kevin asked as we climbed the wooden stairway to the second deck. Opening to the ocean wind, this deck offered doorways that led deeper into the ship. Beyond the rail, brown smog blurred the skyscrapers of Long Beach.

The wind whipped against my cheeks. I pulled my long hair out of my mouth. "A friend once took a picture in a graveyard of this gnarled oak tree with a trunk that had been torn open by a fire. When he had the picture developed, you could see a little boy in nineteenth-century clothes standing in the trunk." We stood by a large, round porthole, glass cracked and dusty. Violence. Neglect. I closed my eyes. "I feel something here. Take a picture of me."

Click-whirr.

Clouds dusted the cobalt blue sky stretching over the upper deck. Kevin took more photos of me beneath cross-shaped, white metal masts. We moved back down onto the second deck, venturing into narrow passages that wound into the heart of the ship. The captain's quarters, the radio room with a thousand knobs and wooden drawers, the steerage, and a first class passenger's cabin recreated as it was on this once-glamorous cruise ship. We took photos of them, hoping that past inhabitants would materialize in the pixels.

The notoriously haunted boiler room was sadly closed for repairs.

We returned to the ship's lobby, exhausted. Unable to get cell reception, Kevin ducked into an Art Deco phone booth to return a call from his band's manager. I sank onto one of the couches with brass piping and ruby velvet fabrics, fleur-de-lis designs cut into the weave. My heart palpitated as I watched Kevin in the booth.

But then my thoughts blurred like static from a radio tuner and an old song swelled from my throat – "Cheek to Cheek" from the movie *Top Hat*, I think – the brilliant lobby acoustics flooding the ship's corridors. The song filled me completely, although I was unsure how I knew it so well. Kevin stepped out of the phone booth, jaw slack, as he watched me sweep through the lobby like Ginger Rogers. I collapsed on the velvet cushions.

"I didn't know you knew 'Cheek to Cheek'," Kevin said. "Or that you could even sing."

"Me, neither," I replied, breathless. "How'd it sound?"

"Terrific! Astounding, even."

"That's good, because I think everyone in Long Beach heard me."

Hungry from the hunt, we returned to the first deck for a meal at one of the onboard restaurants. Pristine white cloths covered the tables, the sun heating the window at our elbows. As we waited for our food, Kevin's distracted look made my heart pound. "This was a great idea. I love this ship," he said. He then leveled those azure eyes at me, direct and serious. "There's something I've been wanting to tell you." A pause. "I'm going to ask Alisa to marry me. I think I want to get married here."

Blackness broke across my eyes, white tablecloth turning to slate.

So sad, so fresh, the days that are no more.

Congratulations and hugs exchanged, we parted outside my apartment complex. In the emptiness of the elevator, I caved to grief.

Eep! Eeeep!

Hermes twittered when I entered, fluttering a little one-legged dance of joy. So much happiness made it hard to cry, but I managed. Sobbing, I carried his cage into the bedroom, where I fed and medicated him. I went to bed, sliding under layers of misery. His cage sat uncovered on the dresser. I lay there with my eyes closed, chest burning with grief.

Someone sat down on the bed beside me.

Electricity scorched my arms and face as my heart kicked into high-speed. When I was a child, after my beloved grandmother died, I sometimes felt the bed depress beside me at night. Eyes closed, I strongly believed it was her spirit comforting me, my guardian angel.

But this felt sinister. Something told me I should, for my life's sake, open my eyes...

Thicker and darker than shadow, the silhouette of a man's body stood out starkly against the Hollywood lights leaking through the window blinds. His fedora's wide brim sliced through the glow as he looked me over, his shoulders squared off in a tailored 1930s suit. But his face was utter pitch.

Hermes screeched in his cage, banging against his water dish as he gyred wildly. I could have sworn his cries were *echoing* —

Startled, the man turned towards Hermes. He then leapt to his feet and fled to a corner of the room where he dove into the darkness.

What are ghosts? And what do they want? Why are they here? Aren't they tied to certain places? I worried that I'd attracted something from the ship. In addition to the nightly visits from Grandma, I'd had many minor encounters with the supernatural since I was a child: spooky coincidences, premonitions, a ghostly sighting at an old building in our neighborhood. I'd never been afraid of it, but this encounter scared me badly.

Fortunately, he didn't return.

Over the next few months, I tried to let go of Kevin. I never told him about my "visitor." When he found an undeniable image on one of the photos where I'd stood beneath a broken ship lamp, he shuffled it away without a word. It broke my heart all over again. Kevin had romanticized the supernatural to such a degree that the real thing seemed indecent. Faulty tarot readings retained passable elements of spirit dealings without exposing anyone to deeper possibilities. Perhaps it was just as well that we weren't together. It still hurt, though. Like by denying evidence of the spirit realm he was also denying me.

Hermes perched on the headboard of my bed at night, head tucked in a wing, a dark sentinel. A month after the "visitation," he lost his down and could fly short distances. The veterinarian took off the bandage, but the medication continued.

Instead of jaunts with Kevin, I spent afternoons in Griffith Park trying to coax Hermes to fly away with other crows. He seemed strong and healthy enough as he swooped around my small apartment. It didn't seem right to keep him. But every time he lifted off my arm and sailed up into the trees, I'd say goodbye and turn away, only for his claws to clasp my shoulder seconds later.

Bringing dates to the apartment proved disastrous. Hermes would launch an airborne fecal assault them, targeting noses, beards and treasured leather jackets. Hermes had learned a few swear words, as well, repeating them with unholy clarity as he attacked. I scolded him, apologizing to my guest, but privately I praised him for loving me so much.

One night in September, he flew straight into the bookcase. "Psychopomp, huh?" my date laughed. "Shoulda just called him 'Psycho.'"

I kicked the bastard out. I then picked up Hermes, stroking his head feathers as he clasped my wrist. He turned an eye up at me like he did that day I first found him. That's when I noticed it:

Those inky eyes were turning milky white.

An emergency visit to the bird vet revealed what I'd feared. The medication was blinding him.

He could only see shadows now.

The wedding took place one cool Los Angeles evening. The way a funeral helps us accept a death, maybe seeing Kevin married would help me finally let go. I wore a long, velvet violet dress I'd found at an antique shop. Long folds of fabric gathered at the small of my back before falling to the floor at my heels. My black hair curled into long Marcel waves draped over my shoulders.

Fearing I'd attract another ghost, I took an oath: *No singing.*

When I arrived at the Queen Mary, signs ushered the guests to a small chapel in a section of the ship that housed a hotel. I noticed that, unlike the tourist section with its tiered decks, the railings on this side of the ship dropped straight down over the water. I felt the height of the towering ship for the first time.

Kevin hurried towards me in a black crushed velvet frock coat, velvet pants and leather boots.

"Carrine! You look stunning!"

Embarrassment heated my cheeks. "Thanks. You look...amazing."

The statement fell like roses at his feet. He bowed deeply and thanked me. "There's something you must know." He pulled me close. "In the reception hall there's a picture in the mural that's the spitting image of you. It's incredible! You have to see it."

I assured him I'd look for it. With that, he smiled again and paused awkwardly, eyes lost in mine. Unable to resist the opportunity with him that close, I kissed him — quickly, like a cousin. And he returned it. "Good luck," I said.

He didn't need it. The wedding unfolded smoothly — from the opening organ concerto, to the string trio played by The Wicker Man and the touching vows written by both bride and groom. Alisa was...well, as pretty as anyone can be in white. When the bride and groom kissed, my heart dropped into my stomach.

It was done.

Dusk washed over the deck. The guests herded around the prow's bend to the reception hall. Inside, name cards stood on a large table near the door, indicating where the respective owners were to sit.

Nested beside a pillar, my table housed all the other "spooks" like me. One angry-looking young man with spiky bleached hair and orange sunglasses gripped an unlit clove cigarette as he debated tersely with an overweight man in a black suit.

"Bowie," the bleached young man snarled.

"Meatballs," the black suit man insisted.

"Bowie!"

"*Meatballs!*"

Another young man with Robert Smith hair and black lipstick stared at the ceiling as a young woman with a black bob chattered next to him. To the right of them was a young man with creamy skin wearing black sunglasses and a blue dinner jacket with a napkin sign tucked into his shirt that he'd drawn with a red ballpoint. It said, "Not A Goht."

I sat across from him. "Not a goat?"

He lowered his glasses and looked at me for a moment with stunning topaz eyes. "Not a *goth*," he said.

"It says 'goat.'"

"Gah! Damned dyslexia!" He crumpled and tossed the napkin. It landed somewhere in the center aisle.

After the food arrived, Goat Boy regaled me with his rigorous literary analysis of John Cale lyrics and random cultural commentary. When the monologue turned to Tim Powers and how *Anubis Gates* had influenced him to study Egyptian hieroglyphs, he must have finally noticed my flagging resolution against throttling him because he shut up.

Is this what I was doomed to? Why couldn't anyone here be more like Kevin?

I was fretting about Hermes being alone and obsessing on the final ceremony kiss when I remembered what Kevin told me. My eyes swept the mural. Chorus lines. Trapeze artists. Equestrian acrobats. A wash of daffodil-yellow paint. Nothing resembled me.

Silver rang against wine glasses. Both families gave very touching toasts and then Kevin's band played raucous drinking songs that brought us all to our feet. As we thundered on the wooden dance floor, I wondered if The Wicker Man would sink the Queen Mary.

Five dances later, I was out of breath and sweaty. I wandered barefoot to our table, but stopped suddenly in the aisle.

Turning end-over-end like tumbleweed, Goat Boy's crumpled napkin crept toward the pillar.

The entire reception faded behind me as I watched it. Mesmerized, I followed.

Behind the pillar, on the mural, seated in an opera balcony — every feature flawlessly replicated — was a painting of *me*.

I ran out of the reception. Behind me in the hall, The Wicker Man's fiddles and drums played merrily. I stopped at the railing overlooking the black waters, rippling with lights under the indigo sky.

The music changed.

Muted trumpets. Strings. Reedy wind instruments. A couple staggered out of the hall and away down the deck. The woman had an hourglass figure, wore a pillbox hat and fur. The man wore a suit and fedora.

Silhouetted from behind by the hall lights, another man in suit and fedora exited the hall and walked towards me, hands cupped over a cigarette as he lit it. His heavy shoes clapped against the deck as he shoved one hand into his slacks pocket and tossed the burnt match with the other. He sidled up beside me at the railing.

"So, doll," he sneered, cigarette between his fingers, "tired of your wedding already?" Salty brown eyes with long lashes, a well-shaped mouth that pouted when he kissed the cigarette butt, and a sharp chin. He tipped back the fedora with a flick of his finger. "Aren't you afraid?"

"Afraid of what?" I asked, trembling. Was I dreaming? What had happened to the band? The ship — ?

"You know what I mean, you little *bitch*!"

"What — ?"

With crippling strength, he grabbed my wrist. "So that's your game, pretending there's nothing between us?" His smelled of cigarettes, onions and cologne.

"Let me go!" Vertigo overwhelmed me as he pressed me against the railing.

"I've waited a long time for this," he said.

"Carrine?" Kevin staggered onto the deck, half-drunk. The strange music continued behind him. "What's going on? Who's he?"

"Here's your *hubby*. Let's tell him we've been screwing, shall we?" the man cried.

"KEVIN!"

Kevin screamed my name, running towards me. The railing cut into my stomach and struck my hipbone as the fedora man swept me up and over. The world upended. Blackness rippled oily with starlight as I tumbled in the cold air.

My face was wet before I struck the water, pain shattering my body. When I broke the icy surface, I heard the rustling, cawing cloud of black feathers above me. *They've come for me*, I thought as my chest caved inward from the pressure, my body swallowed whole by the biting waters. *They've come to guide my soul to the underworld.*

Sirens shrieked as the ambulance sped me to the hospital. My eyes opened to a paramedic and Kevin beside my stretcher.

Kevin kissed my forehead, crushed velvet pants and shirt torn, face bruised, a blanket wrapped around his shoulders. "Thank God you're awake! How do you feel?"

My bottom lip pulled aside, making a "like hell" face, body aching. I then whispered hoarsely, throat raw from coughing up water. "Did they catch him?"

He leaned close with that same urgency as before. The paramedic gave him a warning look, but he continued. "The...man...punched me when I tried to jump overboard to save you." Kevin shook. "But when the birds flew overhead...he *vanished*.""

"The birds?" My bottom lip trembled. "*The crows?*"

Kevin looked as though he'd cry — something I'd never seen him do. We then had a silent conversation with our eyes, where he seemed to confess his newfound terror. He would never accept what had happened. My feelings for Kevin then wavered like smoke and, in a quiet moment, parted sweetly.

The crows.

When I got home, the door stood open to my apartment. My tall blond apartment manager stood inside with three workmen. "The spa upstairs was leaking into your walls — Damn! You look like shit, girl! You okay?"

"Hermes!" I called, searching the rooms. My heart thudded painfully when I found nothing but damp walls and ruined carpet. "Hermes!"

"Uh, Carrine? About the bird..." The apartment manager appeared embarrassed. "We didn't know he was in here. He flew straight out the door hours ago. I think he went over the building gates." He paused. "Like he was in a hurry."

I stared down the empty hall, heartsick. My blind bird. He could have only made such a journey lead by powerful unseen forces. Yet I knew where he went. Who he had taken. And who, because of love, he'd flown to save...

...deep as love;

Deep as first love, and wild with all regret.
O Death in Life, the days that are no more.
The days that are no more.

DARLING
Max Booth III

Max Booth III is the author of *Toxicity*, *The Mind is a Razorblade*, and *How to Successfully Kidnap Strangers*. He's the Editor-in-Chief of *Perpetual Motion Machine Publishing* and an ongoing columnist at Litreactor.com. He works as a hotel night auditor in a small town outside San Antonio, TX. Follow him on Twitter @GiveMeYourTeeth and visit him at talesfromthebooth.com.

Anne caught the hotel creep staring at her through the window. He stood outside in the parking lot under a lamppost, hands shoved into his trouser pockets. He stared up into her room and locked eyes with her. Even from the fifth floor, she felt trapped—violated. As her face twisted in repulsion, his lips spread wider into a smile.

She pulled the curtains shut and spun around, itching like her skin was infested with a colony of ants. A shower. She needed a shower.

"You all right?" Stuart said from the bed, playing with his phone.

"Not really." She glanced over her shoulder at the now closed window. *Is he still out there? Can he see me?*

"What's wrong, babe?"

"That guy from the front desk."

Stuart shook his head, amused, like her discomfort was some kind of joke. "So he touched your hand when he gave you the keys. Some people are just friendly. It's not like he felt you up or anything."

"No. He was just outside…watching me."

Stuart looked up from his phone. "What are you talking about?"

"He's out in the parking lot, right now, just staring up at our window." She pointed. "When he saw I caught him, he started smiling, like it turned him on."

"Babe, there's no way he can see us from down there."

"He saw *me*."

"Well, were you naked?"

"No…"

"Then who cares?"

"*I* do—and you should, too. I think he was masturbating."

Stuart laughed. "He was not masturbating."

Her fists tightened at the sound of his patronizing laughter. "His hands were in his pockets. He could've been."

He laid his phone down and sat up. "Okay, what is your deal today?"

"What is that supposed to mean?"

"You know exactly what that means. You've been freaking out about crazy shit all day. First the gas pumps didn't smell like gas pumps 'should smell', then the billboards were moving when you weren't looking."

"They were."

"However that's possible."

"I don't care what you think is and isn't possible. I know what I saw."

"Babe, don't get mad, but I have to ask."

"Don't you dare."

"Have you stopped taking your medication?"

"Oh, you asshole."

"It's just the doc—"

"Shut up. Just…shut up." Anne looked outside again. The hotel clerk was still under the lamppost, only now his hands were no longer in his pockets but shoved down the front of his trousers. She screamed and pointed at the window as she backpedaled.

"What?" Stuart stood up.

"He-he's out there, *tou-touching* himself."

She sat on the bed, trembling as he rushed to the window and tore open the curtain. He pressed his face against the glass.

"Anne, there's nobody out here."

A knock erupted from the door and they both flinched.

"Front desk," a voice said from the hallway.

Stuart gave her a familiar look—the one that expressed his immense regret at marrying a psychopath—and answered the door. Anne peeked around the closet wall. The night creep stood in the hallway, wearing the same smile he'd had on in the parking lot while pleasuring himself.

Stuart leaned against the doorframe. Was he blocking Anne's view of the creep who was disturbing her, or was he blocking the creep's view of his insane and embarrassing wife?

"Can we help you with anything?" Stuart asked, and Anne felt the rage bubble up. *Can we help you with anything?* Not *What the hell do you think you're doing with my wife?* No. Instead he wanted to *help* the sicko.

The night clerk's voice was just as nasally as it had been during check-in. "Yes, sir, terribly sorry to bother you at this hour, but I've seemed to run into a rather peculiar situation."

"What's that?"

"Well, it's the darnedest thing, but I've gotten some complaints from the floor below you about a leak."

"A leak?"

"Uh-huh. I went into their room and sure enough, there's water spreading in their ceiling."

"Huh. Well, there's nothing in our room. Must be from somewhere else."

"Surely, sir, surely. However, I'm afraid I must insist on double-checking."

Anne's chest tightened. *Tell him no.*

"Okay, I guess that's fine."

Anne frantically crawled to the front of the bed and pressed her back against the wall as she wrapped the comforter around her body. Despite being fully dressed, she felt naked with him in the room. The comforter did not offer much protection. A musky layer of sickening dirt penetrated her flesh as he entered. His footsteps were soft and thunderous. They went into the bathroom, sparing Anne from another glance at the hotel creep's pale, nauseating face.

She overheard Stuart mumbling something about pipes and toilets and the hotel clerk laughed. The sound of his laughter traveled through her like poison in her veins. How could Stuart be cracking jokes? How could he be taking this so lightly? He didn't believe her. He *never* believed her. He thought the gas smell was silly, he thought the billboards were silly, and now he thought the perverted hotel creep was silly. Everything was always so silly.

"Might as well check the rest of the room, if you don't mind."

"No, go right ahead. We don't mind."

Anne shrunk as they exited the bathroom. Stuart ignored her completely, but the hotel creep couldn't seem to take his eyes off her.

"Hello, ma'am. It's a real pleasure to see you again."

She said nothing, just stared at him and wished him out of existence.

"I apologize for my wife. She isn't feeling too well."

She wanted to protest, but she couldn't find the strength. The way the hotel creep stared at her made her feel like an experiment in some scientist's laboratory. Studying her, examining every inch of her flesh. The comforter around her body might as well be translucent for all the security it provided.

"Feeling a bit under the weather, are we, darling?" he said, and she had to swallow a mouthful of vomit. He waited for a response. She gave him none. He shrugged.

The hotel creep bent down and pressed his hand against the carpet. Perhaps he was feeling for wet patches in the floor—or, more realistically, only pretending to check for wet patches to avoid suspicion from her husband. If that was the case, he was wasting his time. The only person in the world Stuart didn't trust was his own wife.

"Hmm," the hotel creep said. "Doesn't seem to be wet. I guess the leak must be coming from another room, after all."

"I hope it doesn't continue spreading," Stuart said.

"You and I both, sir." The hotel creep paused, his attention caught on something next to the bed. That repugnant smile returned as he leaned down and scooped something up. He glanced at Anne. "Darling, I believe you've misplaced something."

He extended his hand and presented a pill bottle with her name on the label. Her medication. The real enemy. It must've fallen out of her purse. He remained kneeled next to the bed, holding out the bottle, waiting for her to take it. She didn't want to. She just wanted him to leave and never look at her again. But that wasn't going to happen until she reached out and grabbed the bottle.

Anne bit her lower lip and wrestled a shaking arm from under the comforter. She moved it slowly forward, fingers stretching. Just as they curled around the top of the pill bottle, the hotel creep shoved it into her palm and enclosed her entire hand with his own. Lightning shot through her insides. The hotel creep no longer smiled but instead gritted his teeth together, the same way a wild dog might moments before chomping down on its prey. Time paused as their hands connected. She wanted to pull her arm back but couldn't remember how to control her motor functions.

Then she realized the hotel creep's eyes were changing colors.

They hadn't *changed* from one color to another. They were *changing* colors. *Colors*, plural. Blue, green, brown, red, black, blue, green, brown, red, black.

Like someone was flipping through television channels and couldn't settle on a program.

Anne screamed. The hotel creep jumped to his feet and backed away. "Terribly sorry, miss, didn't intend to startle you."

"Get out," she said. "Get the hell out."

"Yes, ma'am, right away."

He headed for the door. Stuart walked him out and apologized for his wife's behavior. "Like I said, she's very unwell tonight."

"Quite understandable, sir. No worries."

Once the door was closed, Stuart stormed back to the bed and pointed at the pill bottle in her hand. "I'm going to tell you this once more. Take your medication. Otherwise I'm finding the next hospital and admitting you."

Anne looked at the pill bottle, then at her husband. But was he her husband? How well did she even know this man?

"Babe, take the medication. Please."

The hotel phone rang on the nightstand. She dropped the pill bottle on the mattress and raised the phone to her ear by instinct. If she had stopped to consider who would be calling the hotel at this time of night—not to mention the fact that nobody even knew they were staying here—she would have not only ignored the ringing, but also ripped the phone's cord from the wall.

But that didn't occur to her until she said, "Hello?" and only heard deep, heavy breathing on the other end.

"Hello?"

Breathing.

"I'm talking to your manager in the morning, just so you know," she said. "So have fun while it lasts, pervert."

The breathing stopped. "The fun is only just beginning, darling."

Anne threw the phone across the room. It soared over Stuart's head and exploded against the wall.

"Jesus Christ," Stuart said. "Who was that?"

"Who do you think?"

"The front desk guy?"

She nodded. "Your new best friend."

"What did he want?"

"That he was going to kill me."

Stuart brushed his hands through his hair. "What did he really say?"

"I'm done talking to you, Stu. I'm done."

"Good. At this point, I could use a break from crazy."

"You're such a bastard."

"But remember what I said." He held up his finger. "Don't think I'm bluffing about the hospital."

Anne snarled. "You try touching me and I'll rip out your jugular."

He stared at her, dumbstruck. She wasn't joking. She was so sick of his aura. His spoiled, decomposing, stupid aura.

Stuart grabbed his cell phone and left the room. Good. She hoped he never came back. She lay down on the bed and tried to control her breathing. Her weight sank into the mattress and the pill bottle rolled and touched her arm, burning her skin like a crucifix pressed against a vampire. The medication, always the damn medication. Whenever anything went wrong in her life, everybody always said it could be solved by popping another pill into her mouth. She didn't trust the medication. The medication lied to her. It told her things were okay when they were far from it. The medication made her ignorant of reality. It veiled her perspective with a Disney-themed filter.

She threw the bottle across the room and closed her eyes. When she opened them again, three hours had passed. Stuart was still gone. Maybe he really had left her for good. That wouldn't be such a bad thing, right? She could survive on her own. Anne wasn't weak. Anne could do whatever she wanted. She didn't need a husband and she sure as hell didn't need medication.

Still, though. They were in the middle of nowhere. What if he had left her here? She was two states away from home. What was she supposed to do?

His cell phone went straight to voicemail. She considered leaving a message, maybe apologize, but she couldn't think of a valid reason. If anything, *she* was the one owed an apology.

She pulled back the curtain half-expecting to find the hotel creep pleasuring himself in the parking lot again, but the night held not a soul. Their car was still outside, however, so Stuart hadn't gone too far. He was probably down in the lobby, complaining about his crazy wife.

But for three hours?

Acidic saliva bubbled in her throat. Three hours were more than enough time to relieve stress. He should have been back by now. They had to wake up early to hit the road. They had to get home. She tried his phone again. Straight to voicemail. She called the front desk, but it just rang and rang.

She did not want to leave the room. She did not want to go down to the lobby. This was Stuart's fault. He was doing this on purpose, making her put her shoes on and ride the elevator down to the first floor. He knew she hated hotel creep. This was all a game to him. A big, ugly joke.

The lobby was just as empty as the parking lot. She roamed the dining area and the hallways. Only herself and the ghosts. She anticipated the hotel creep springing from one of the rooms as she passed and dragging her inside with him. Where else could he be? How could both her husband and the hotel creep be missing? They had to be together. Maybe they were outside, smoking cigarettes. She stared at the front entrance and considered further exploring the parking lot, but couldn't muster up the courage. She was not going outside at three-thirty in the morning. Maybe she was crazy, but she definitely wasn't stupid.

Five minutes later she was back in bed. Her heart was beating too violently to even entertain the concept of sleep. Where the hell was Stuart? She tried calling again. Voicemail. This time she left a message.

"Hey…I don't know where you are, but it's getting late. I'm sorry we were fighting. I'm worried, okay? Please come back."

Before she could set the phone down, it began ringing in her hand.

INCOMING CALL: STU

She answered it and heard screaming. Screaming so loud she had to distance the cell phone from her ear. She raised the phone to her mouth and whispered, "St-Stu? What's happening?"

The phone went dead.

Above her, a series of bangs crashed against the ceiling. Something was going wild in the room above her. Anne called the front desk, intent on issuing a complaint, but again nobody answered. She hung up on the ninth ring.

The banging from above not only continued, but increased in volume. Someone was performing construction, maybe. At this time? No. Something bad was happening up there. That, or someone was having a little too good of a time. Either way, it was something she didn't want to be involved with.

Dust fell as the ceiling shook. *What if whoever's up there falls through?*

She glanced at the hotel phone, then at the ceiling. The cell phone was still in her hand. Had she imagined the phone call? That hadn't been Stuart screaming. Nobody had been screaming. This was all in her head. Just another episode. Another tragic breakdown in the life of Anne Harris. One for the books.

The banging had grown so loud she couldn't even hear herself think.

She put her shoes back on and stormed to the elevator. She searched for the sixth floor button, but the panel ended at floor five, which was *her* floor. She stepped back out of the elevator, shaking, mind racing a mile per second. She scanned the ceiling of the hallway, trying to piece together a puzzle that was never meant to be solved.

The roof. The banging is coming from the roof.

Stuart.

Anne raced down the hallway. She pushed open the entrance to the stairway and climbed the last set of steps. The door to the roof was propped open, like it was expecting Anne's arrival.

Welcome to the show, darling.

The ground made sticky noises as she stepped forward, and when she looked down, the cement was covered in a dark, reddish liquid.

Blood. The cement is covered in blood.

Up ahead, Stuart sat slouched against an air vent. His stomach was a mess of spilled organs. She rushed toward him, sobbing. In one hand he held his cell phone. In the other he held his tongue.

what the hell what the hell oh my god what the hell is happening

Something screamed from the opposite end of the roof. Anne stood and peeked around the air vent, whimpering, trembling, on the edge of total collapse. The hotel creep knelt on his knees in the center of the roof. He was naked and soaked in blood. Her husband's blood. He held up something the size of a softball, dripping of gore.

it's a heart oh my god he's holding a heart he's holding my husband's heart Stu Stu please god no this can't be happening please make it stop

The hotel creep didn't seem to notice her presence. Everything in her told her to run while she still had a chance to make it out alive, but she couldn't move. Her feet had melted into the cement, into the pool of her husband's infinite blood.

The hotel creep bit into the heart. Its juices poured down his face, into his mouth. He licked it up like a dog in the desert. She watched him devour her husband's heart.

He screamed louder now and thrashed on the ground, hugging his chest and grinding his nails into his shoulders. He arched his back and cried like he was the one being tortured, like he was the one who'd had all his organs ripped out of his stomach.

Then he started tearing his skin off.

Almost like it was made of Velcro. One strip at a time. Beneath the flesh—blood and tissue. More flesh. She watched the hotel creep scream and mutilate himself and all she could do was cry with him.

what is happening

When he'd finished with his body, he reached one bloody hand up to his face and pulled that off as well. Just a mask. Everything was a mask. She understood this now. Nothing was real. Nothing was ever real.

Underneath the hotel creep's mask, he wore a mask that resembled her now dead husband's face. Not just resembled. It was an exact replica.

He collapsed on the roof, still crying, still hugging himself.

"Anne!" the hotel creep shouted. "Anne! I know you're out here. Help me. Please. It hurts so much. Oh god, Anne."

Anne turned around and fled the roof. The hotel creep continued screaming her name, but she tried her best to block out his voice. This wasn't happening. Stuart had been right. She should've taken her medication. When she was off her meds, reality disintegrated. Her husband wasn't really dead. He was probably still outside, having a smoke. He'd be back up to their room any moment now, and when he did, she would be in bed, ready to apologize, ready to tell him how she'd been an idiot and how much she loved him.

The pill bottle was still on the floor where she'd thrown it. She took triple the prescribed dosage and wrapped herself up with the comforter, not caring if she was covered in her husband's blood, not caring if the sky was crashing or if the hotel no longer existed or if anything really existed. All that mattered was she was back in bed and nobody or nothing could take that from her.

Anne woke up in her husband's arms. Stuart was already awake, smiling at her.

"Sleep well, darling?"

She rubbed her forehead. "I've slept better."

"I'm sorry to hear that. But hey, you can sleep more in the car if you want. I've already packed us all up."

Anne returned a smile. "I might take you up on that."

In the lobby, Anne approached the front desk to drop off their keys.

The clerk—a woman now—was on the phone, so she just laid them down on the counter.

"I know, I know," the woman said, "but I'm telling you, he isn't here. I've looked everywhere. No, no, the register isn't missing anything. He's just...gone."

Stuart pulled up front and Anne got in the passenger's seat. Before she buckled her seatbelt, she started digging through her purse.

"Everything all right, darling?"

She pulled out her pill bottle and unscrewed the lid. "Yes, honey. Everything is perfect."

"Brilliant." He caressed her cheek, smiling at her. Had his eyes always been so dark? "You know I love you, right, darling?"

Anne tossed a couple pills in her mouth and dry-swallowed them. "I love you, too."

CATHOLIC GUILT
Ryan Bradley

Ryan Bradley has published work in *The Missouri Review*, *The Rumpus*, *Pinball*, the anthology *Drawn to Marvel*, and others, as well as winning the 2015 JP Reads flash fiction contest and contributing regularly to *Action Figure Fury*. He will receive his MFA from Emerson College in May.

I'm lying in the dark, wondering how my mother managed to convince me to come on yet another one of these family vacations, and why I hadn't just taken a wine cooler and sat down at the kid's end of the table when the music starts in the parlor. Toccata en Fugue in D minor. The haunted house song. Of course. I want it to be one of my uncles screwing with me. My mom was the oldest and she had me young, so they're actually closer to my age, twenty-three, than to hers, and they used to save their boogers on index cards and chase me around, so I wouldn't put it past them, sneaking down from the bedrooms while their wives try to sleep and putting on this creepy ass organ music.

What I don't get is how they'd be willing to freak out their own kids just to scare me. Out of my mom's five brothers, maybe two are decent dads, but even the other three don't want to deal with their beautiful children (whose genes no doubt come from their wonderful mothers, because no nibbling has seemed to catch any part of the jerkoff gene that infects their fathers) running into their beds and blocking their vacation sex, which I heard one of them bragging to the rest could possibly be oral.

The way the house is laid out, I'm sleeping across the hall from the kitchen. The hall goes down the side of the dining room, which, by grandma's decree, has a big enough table to sit all twenty-three of us without a separate kid's table. The dining room connects to the kitchen on one side, and a parlor on the other. There's a swinging door between the kitchen and the dining room, and a sliding one at the parlor. The stereo with it's spooky scary Sebastian Bach is on that far end, and my youngest

Uncle, Alex, has closed every door in the house because his one-year-old, Elizabeth the cutest damn girl in the world, loves doing naked laps but can't reach door knobs yet. I can either walk down the hallway for the length of an Olympic-sized pool, or I play the game of opening three doors and scare the piss out of myself three times.

The thing is, I don't want anyone with an ounce of my blood in their veins to see me in the gym shorts and tank top I sleep in and I couldn't turn back in the hallway if someone else is coming to investigate. I'd have to press on and pretend like I don't know that they're thinking of course Janie's daughter (Did you know she was born out of wedlock? The scandal!) doesn't sleep in a nightgown like a proper lady.

So I go through the first door, into the kitchen, and I leave the light off. My eyes are adjusted to the dark, and if it is an uncle screwing with me, and I come from this side I might manage to scare him instead.

The kitchen's got a granite island covered in an excessive amount of knives. Like, seriously. Whoever stocked this place must have wanted to have enough knives that they could stab every guest with their own individualized blade. There is no other possible explanation for a house having so many knives.

I put a hand on the island and follow it to the door to the dining room, and all the time this Johann joker's getting louder. The air conditioning's chilled the tile floor, and granite, so I'm getting goosebumps all over. I'm trying to play it in my head like I'm getting closer, and that's why it sounds louder, not that it's being turned up because someone would need to be able to sense me through three closed doors to change the volume as I get closer.

That's when ye olde Catholic programming kicks in, and I'm saying Hail Marys under my breath, and thinking about how mad I'll be in the morning for falling back into religion. Forgive me, it's been thirteen months since my last regression.

Here's the thing about being raised Catholic, you can be an atheist for a decade, read the complete works of Nietzsche, and defecate on the steps of a Church, but when everything goes to crap you're back praying to the Sweet Lord Baby Jesus. They programmed you. It starts age three or so with people teaching you that if you think a set of words, you don't even need to say them aloud, an all-powerful being is going to pop down and intercede on your behalf. That toy you wanted? Yours. The bully from the school bus? Smote. Whatever you want, you say enough Our Fathers and Hail Marys and it will be yours, and you don't need to do a thing to achieve it. And here I am, in a rented mansion in Cape Cod, with twenty-three of my mother's ass-hat relatives praying that it is a living, flesh and bones, non-ethereal being who turned on the stereo.

I don't like my odds.

I put my hand on the door to the dining room. It's a butler's door, so the Colonel, a Union general in the Civil War according to our travel agent, could have food in and out as fast as possible while still not having to linger with the help. It can swing all the way open into either room and it moves at the slightest touch. I peak through the crack, making sure an Uncle or something else isn't there to jump out at me, but I can't see much.

I've got a view of the back of the Colonel's chair. There's a dresser that's filled with silverware and fine china on the left. Everything is made of oak, and the corners have been carved into flowery vines and buds. These little flourishes make people like my grandmother, born in Irish Boston, feel like they've made it. There's a silver mirror above the dresser, but I only catch the edge of it, not enough to get the rest of the room in the reflection.

I let the door swing back toward me, but stop it from coming back into the kitchen. Who or whatever is working the stereo isn't going to see me.

I hit the door open a little farther. This time I get three and a half seats, including the head of the table. They're empty. The door that leads from the hallway into that side of the dining room is on the right. It's closed, and I'm glad because if it were open I'm sure there'd be something going past it in the corner of my eye as soon as I passed it.

I plunge through, into the dining room. I say a Hail Mary. I walk around the table on the opposite side of the door. I want to be as far from any entry point as possible. What I really want is to be safe, curled up in bed, with a sheet, preferably a quilt in this air conditioning, pulled up to my chin but Bach has gotten even louder and I'm sure it's not the diminishing number of doorways between me and the stereo. The jumps it's making are too loud.

The doors to the parlor come into view. They're heavy sliders, and I realized that I won't be able to push them open quietly. I wish I was back in bed, again, and I tell Jesus—who I'd like to believe in only as a historical figure—that I'd like his intercession in the matter of the haunted stereo.

I touch the wooden top of each chair as I go by. Running my hand across something smooth, the calm of finished carpentry, soothes me as much as I can be soothed. I wonder why I don't give up. With Bach getting louder someone else will hear and turn off the damned stereo. Maybe I keep going because if it's my Uncles they will smell my fear in the morning. Maybe I go because my cousins will get woken up and as much as I hate my uncles, I love their children even more. Maybe I go because need to know exactly what is working the stereo and at some level I believe that if I can prove it is an electronic problem or a manmade disturbance I can return back to my unspiritual life. I don't know why I do the things that I do, and I suspect that the people who believe they do are lying to themselves.

Another Hail Mary. I'm at the sliding doors now. I put my ear to them, and the ever-louder fugue is too loud for me to hear if anything is moving in the room. Or maybe everything is still. I can't tell.

I press my finger into the cracks between the doors. I don't know what I'm hoping to find, what I'm expecting. In chaos there is infinite possibility, but all probability points to this being a prank. I believe that the world is chaos. Maybe it's "believed" now. Past tense.

Here I am, praying, terrified, and opening the door. Was this what my mother was hoping for when she told me this vacation would give me a chance to bond?

The doors creak loudly. In a leather armchair, there is a woman I have never seen before. She doesn't turn at the squeals of the runner. Her hair is short, and seems to be blonde and white all at once. Her legs are folded. When I get the doors all the way open, she looks up at me and it's as though an ice cube has been stuffed down the back of my shirt. We make eye contact. Hers are green, but as I look into them, I can see the red, white, and blue of the flag blanket hanging over the back of the chair. I can see through her. I'm too afraid to move. I feel as though I'm going to vomit.

"You're not my husband," she says.

I shake my head no. I almost motormouth, and tell her that I'm not anyone's husband. Tell her I like her dress. Thank her for allowing my family into her home so graciously. Ask her if she's a big baroque fan. Ask her how this is happening. I have so many things to say that none can get out.

"I haven't seen him years" she says, wistfully. She rubs at her eye, as though she's been crying. The music is hurting my ears now, but I can hear her perfectly.

"Will you pray with me?" she says.

I nod. What else am I going to do? It's her house. We're just renting it.

She puts her hands on her knees, and rocks forward gently. "It takes me a minute to stand up now," she explains. She's transparent, but I feel her like I've never felt anyone. It's like I've jammed a fork into a socket. She manages to climb out of her chair on the third try, and she reaches out for me.

I know from my great-grandparents that I'm meant to put my arm out here, let her grab my forearm and guide her to her destination. I step back instead, and she falls forward. She is gone before she hits the floor. The stereo shuts off on its own. I shiver. Even with the air conditioning blasting, I shouldn't be this cold. I wonder who she was, and who I am.

BENEATH
J.M. Cole

J.M. Cole's style of writing has been described as "reminiscent of Lovecraft, Stoker and Shelley" a complimentary description for an author who is fascinated by all things 'old and creepy'. A longtime fan of old school horror, J.M. crafts stories meant to provoke a deep carnal fear within the human soul, a fear spawned by the mind's inability to comprehend or accept those things that could not and should not, be. J.M.'s current projects include various short stories, two screenplays, and an ongoing horror anthology.

J.M. Cole lives in beautiful, historical and haunted, Portsmouth, New Hampshire with her daughter, Isa.

He was right...for all his weeping and pleading which had been received upon dismissive ears. It was there, however convinced I was that it was my mind's own, malignant creation. *It was there*, a creeping, preternatural thing, grotesque...abhorrent.

The stench was putrescent. It struck the throat and dripped into the lungs, viscous and clinging. I recalled that reeking smell which had sent me searching...the floors, the ceilings, the walls...the walls...those walls with their scrambling noises. They had spoken as much truth as he had, had begged me to listen as he had, had been disregarded as he had.

It was vermin, vermin which left no filth ridden beds of torn fabric, no holes gnawed into the burlap with spilling cereals. Vermin which did not die despite malicious snares, despite virulent poisons presented as delicacies. Vermin that could make such thundering sounds as to suggest that swarms of them thrived in the tight spaces between the beams. It stuns the mind. How ignorant one can seem when recalling the past.

What hissing breath had coiled against the wall behind the banging of my fist when my frustration brought me to raise it to the mohair and plaster? Had I known...had I known that this...thing...had been the source...what would I have done? What in this moment am I to do with this stinking thing, its twisted body raised inches above the floorboards with its malformed hands pressed against the pine?

And this poor child...this poor, trembling child, who clutches my trousers with knuckles white and a face as pallid as death's hand. This child who had scampered to the edge of my bed every night, sweat beaded upon his brow, tears stained upon his cheeks. With a heart beating eagerly in his chest. I had seen the panting breaths which were as reluctant to give him air as they were to calm the quickened heaving of his lungs.

His frail finger had waivered softly, like a leaf in the night's breeze. His arm was the branch, stiff and immovable but for a slight quaking. He pointed. There had been nothing to account for his fear. This I told him as I returned him to the warmth of his bed, laid him down despite his protests, despite his clinging fingers which pressed so firmly into my flesh that my temper was challenged.

There I left him, my child, the one thing given to me in this world that I cherished above all else. I placed him there with irritation. I calmed him with dismissal. There he laid, his tiny body trembling, his lips uttering weeping gasps as he watched his father's departure, as he watched the door bring the light of the hallway down to a sliver.

There my child lay, listening to the scurrying in the wall, the nearness of it growing. Listening to the horrific scraping of some slithering thing dragging itself up from the darkness, clawing its way free from the damaged wall and its gaping hole which I had so slothfully hidden from the eyes by the use of the boy's bed.

The wretched hands brought with them a hideous scratching. The sound carried to his frightened ears and brought heat to his face...all of these things which he had told me, which I had given to the imagination of a child painting the darkness...I deserve no forgiveness, and to know, to know, that these things were not the entirety of his suffering...

There were periods void of sound, moments where the blissful veil of sleep began to rest upon his eyes...moments stolen by a sudden blow upon the underside of the mattress. I had noted the upset bed on several occasions. It was evident that some movement had caused it to wander from its established place. I thought him a restless sleeper. His bed linens I had seen, even on cold nights, torn from their place, tossed upon the planks as if wantonly discarded. This I took as a result of recurrent nightmares, an assumption which seemed apt by his assertion that a hand had reached up from beneath the bed, a hand which owned gnarled fingers, black as pitch. These, he said, curled upon the bed covers and wrested them from their place leaving him exposed beneath the black eyes of some kneeling thing aside his bed.

He was right...for all his weeping and pleading...it was there, this abomination, this wretch which words could not describe. It was there, staring at me, crouched in the darkness beneath where he slept.

SLURG
Lance Davis

Lance is a married father of 2 from Northwest, AR whose stories and poems have appeared in *Frightmares A Fistful of Flash Fiction, Gothic Blue Book III: The Graveyard Edition, Gothic Blue Book IV: Folklore Edition, Blood Reign Lit, The Twelve Nights of Christmas, Peripheral Distortions by Death Throes Publishing Bones II, Captive Hearts Anthology published by Clouded Tower Press,* and the *Horror Writers Association Poetry Showcase Volume II.* He can be found at: http://www.facebook.com/LanceDavisII.

He parked in the shade of the neon sign that was conveniently facing the street and looked at the black leather bag. Its contents had been weighing heavily on his mind for the past couple of hours and he didn't want to let it out of his sight now. However, not knowing who could be watching, he didn't want to take it in either. He looked past it out the window to the setting sun where shimmering waves of mid-July heat slithered heavenward. He wanted to keep driving but the chances of getting pulled over after dark was slightly higher than through the heat of the day. Besides, he was exhausted.

Seeing no one around, he reluctantly grabbed the bag strap and hauled it out the door behind him then faked a stretch, glancing toward various open windows for signs of nosey travelers. If anyone was here they probably had the blinds drawn and air conditioning on. There wasn't even an eating establishment nearby. Just the old Inn and a stretch of desolate highway.

Hoisting the bag, he headed for the front office with the crunch of parking lot gravel piercing his ears. He knew between his height and build he was an intimidating looking guy and he wanted to do as much as he could to avoid any second glances. As far as anyone needed to know he was just a weary traveler looking for a room.

He opened the office door hoping for a blast of cool air to rush out and welcome his arrival but all he got was the distinctive "ding" announcing him. If anything, it was hotter in here than outside and for a moment he considered returning to his vehicle and heading to the next town.

"Need a room?"

He had been so intent on turning around and leaving that he didn't even notice the guy behind the counter. "The air conditioning broke?" he asked, composing himself and stepping up to the desk. The guy sitting behind the chipped oak counter looked to be only a couple of years younger than himself. However, he was built much smaller with short receding black hair and matching black glasses so thick he couldn't even tell the color of his eyes. The name Benjamin S. Lurgosi was stamped into the small bronze looking pin just below the words True Water Inn.

"Yep," the attendant answered. "A guy would have to be pretty desperate to stay here tonight," he smirked. "The whole place is down."

He considered his options and decided that tonight he was one of those desperate people, but didn't care for the little man's implications, nor the way he kept staring at the bag. "Yeah," he reluctantly answered, "just one night."

Benjamin finally took his eyes off the bag and reached under the desk for a ledger, which he plopped between them. A black Bic rolled out onto the counter. He grabbed it and flipped the book open. "Name?"

"Listen, I'm just going to pay cash."

"Doesn't matter," the attendant cut him off, "I still got to put something."

"Smith, Bill Smith." There was no way he was giving this guy his real name.

Benjamin glanced at the bag again. Bill casually grasped the straps and placed it on the floor out of sight.

"You got a photo I.D. Mr. Smith?"

Bill reached into his pocket and produced two crisp hundred dollar bills. "This should more than cover it and consider the rest yours. There's another hundred if you'll finish filling that out for me."

Benjamin tapped the pen on the counter, then tossed it into the ledger and put it away. When his hands resurfaced he was holding a key.

"I'd like something,"

"Around back," Benjamin finished for him. He jingled the key. "Detached room, end of the parking lot."

"Detached?"

Benjamin smirked again, "Thought you might like the extra privacy. Never know who might show up in the middle of the night."

Bill grabbed the key and the bag strap then turned for the door.

"I believe you said something about another hundred?" Benjamin asked.

Bill grabbed another and flung it on the counter without turning fully around. The greedy little guy had already gotten too good a look at him.

"Have a good night Mr. Smith, and if you need anything just call the front desk and ask for Benny," he said almost too smug in Bill's opinion.

Back outside, the previous heat seemed to have abated in comparison to the furnace of the main office. He hurried to the car and pulled around back looking toward the end of the parking lot. He found a lone bungalow sitting by itself, away from the main unit. If this had been a classy establishment he would've mistaken it for a pool house the way it sat alone in the gravel surrounded by trees.

He parked in the last spot and got out, noticing his was the only vehicle back here. This was perfect, he thought. He could easily see headlights coming and the surrounding foliage gave perfect cover in case he had to get out of here quick. Only when he got inside with his back to the locked door did he begin to relax.

Clutching the bag to his chest he reached out and found the light switch. A single bulb switched on and cast the room in a pale glow. The room was sparse, containing a single queen size bed, a four drawer dresser complete with the smallest television he had seen in years, a small oval desk and of course a bathroom even he wasn't ready to enter yet. The ancient scent of cigarette smoke marinated the atmosphere.

"It's just one night."

He sat on the end of the bed and instantly wondered if it would be better sleeping on this slab of concrete or the brown shag carpeting. He opened the bag on his lap and forgot his worries. The alluring scent of uncounted hundred dollar bills wafted up and filled his senses. After taking a moment to calm himself he reached for the television remote on the nightstand wondering if the robbery had made the news yet. He pressed the power button but nothing happened.

Figures, he thought, dropping the remote. The last thing he wanted to do was call Benny and complain thereby drawing even more unnecessary attention his way. He was too tired to care that much anyway and wondered if sleep would even be possible in this heat. Instead he lay on the bed and contemplated on which direction to head in the morning.

Something moved. He looked at the bare smoke stained partitions searching for an emerging rat or cockroach when something caught his eye. The word Slurg had been carved into the drywall about eye level. The rats moved again. "Going to be a long damn night." He kicked the baseboard and went to the bathroom.

The room was more of a nightmare than he had imagined. The once white tiles were a urine stained yellow, the bathtub was half-full of what looked like dark green swamp water that matched the water in the cracked toilet. He stood before it, his bladder begging to be emptied wondering what the hell it could be. A small green bubble blew up and popped releasing a noxious odor toward the ceiling and almost causing him to release his lunch. He urinated in the corner instead and went to the sink where he cranked on the hot water and waited.

The floor beneath his feet trembled in minute vibrations he presumed to be the pipes awakening after eons of non-use. A small green trickle matching the slime in the toilet and tub issued from the mouth of the faucet then fell like a slug trail and pooled into the sink too thick to continue its path down the drain. Bill cranked the faucet off but it didn't stop the flow. Slowly it filled the basin before coming to a stop along with the vibrations beneath his feet.

He held his hand over it feeling a faint heat. A noxious steam wafted upwards. The pipes trembled again jetting the liquid into the sink and splashing his bare arms. Bill backed away, beating at his appendages like they were on fire. The splotches on his arms ate at his flesh like acid boring into his skin. "The hell with this," he decided.

Back in the bedroom, he tried to ignore the pain in his arms while bundling the money back in the bag. The mice in the walls were back at it, crawling and scraping. "Shut up!" he yelled and kicked the wall. His foot went through and into something soft. He jerked it out and found it covered in slime. The ooze trickled through the newly opened hole like an emerald lava flow. A hundred tiny knives were piercing their way through his hiking boot on their way to his foot. Just outside he heard a voice.

"Throw out the money," the guy yelled.

Bill limped to the window, kicking his shoes off and hoping to be rid of the acidic corrosion eating at his feet. "Benny?"

The young man stood before Bill's car waving his arm. "Throw the money out and come on!"

Bill's mind reeled. He turned to the bed and found the flow continuing to ooze from the hole. It was attaching itself to the bedsheets and crawling up. In the bathroom, it continued to flow from the sink which was overflowing and pooling across the floor. Bill grabbed the rest of the money and threw it in the bag then raced for the door and stopped. The goo was blocking his exit like a solid green curtain.

"Throw it out!" Benny yelled.

Bill took a step back and heaved the bag through then ran to the window. It was sitting on the outside smoking from the acid-like stuff eating through its material. Benny was already racing for it. "Be careful!" Bill warned, but the young man just smiled and grabbed the straps. The goo on the bag blinked out then reappeared under the strange little man's skin. His hand then arm lit up and when he turned, Bill realized his glasses were gone and his dark green eyes seemed to pierce his own like the acidic sting that was now boring into his feet.

The flow at the still open front door was ebbing inside, Bill looked in all directions at once for a way out. A chunk of wall paneling above the headboard chipped away as more of the goo bled through while small droplets fell through cracks in the ceiling toward the floor.

He ripped the heavy blue blanket off the bed and wrapped himself in it. The goo was eating into his right foot and in moments he wasn't sure if he would be able to walk at all. The pain in his arms still begged for attention.

He stood before the front door gathering his nerve while waves of heat emanated from the slime waterfall. Taking a deep breath he covered his head and lurched forward. The fabric surrounding him immediately began to melt. The green tar was eating its way through, trying to reach his skin. He backed into the room and thrust the blanket off his head

"Benny!" he screamed. "Get me out of here!" He didn't think he could walk and refused to look at his feet or arms for fear of seeing a hole through each one. A single slimy drop fell from the ceiling and landed on the back of his head. "Benny!"

He crawled to the window begging for the little man's aide but fearing he already knew better. Outside, Benjamin S. Lurgosi was already a fading green glow disappearing around the corner of the Inn presumably back to his duties at the front desk. He suddenly wondered if one of those duties was luring suckers like himself to the room at the end of the lot.

He frantically searched for a way out of the area as the vile liquid seeped through his skull. The last thing his eyes landed on before the ooze bled through them was the word Slurg that lit up the room like a rusted neon Inn sign, welcoming its desperate travelers.

COLLECTED POEMS
Ashley Dioses

Ashley Dioses' work has been published in *Spectral Realms* No. 1, 2, and 3 by *Hippocampus Press*, *Weird Fiction Review* #5 by *Centipede Press*, *Necronomicum: The Magazine of Weird Erotica* Issue 4 by *Martian Migraine Press*, an upcoming issue of *Xnoybis* from *Dunhams Manor Pres*, and a few amateur ezines. Her debut poetry collection will be published by *Hippocampus Press* in 2016. She has also appeared on Ellen Datlow's full recommended list for Year's Best Horror Vol. 7 for her poem *Carathis*, published in *Spectral Realms* No. 1 by *Hippocampus Press*.

Prelude- My Dark Diary

In my dark diary I speak of things unknown.
The daemons in my mind have now forever tainted
The sirens, pixies, and the vampires there alone.
In my scelestic head, their dooms are ever painted.

My meditations soothe my thoughts yet oft have brought
Grim scenes of death and horrid shadows and red fields,
Where chanting cats of black and butterflies have fought.
Cruel Mother Nature brings dark scenes and never yields.

The many passing centuries have made me weary,
And my still beating heart has grown so hard, so cold.
From his high castle 'that has grown too damp and dreary,'
A Sorcerer begins to speak with words so bold.

He speaks of love and wishes that there was an 'us',
But it has been so long since solitude was broken
That I am torn. My heart and head are making fuss,

Yet his sworn vow of love is offered as his token.

Enough of love—this subject hurts my weary head!
My mind has always had some imperfections, though....
Illusions render one either insane or dead,
And yet created fears allow the mind to grow.

Who knows what happens once the subtle snap occurs
In lurking darkness? Thoughts of surgeries precise,
A taste for human flesh, dark spells.... My vision blurs
As my mind fills with ghastly visions and advice.

Mircalla

The faintest winds of the east, stealthily oft steal
Across the lands of Styria; Hell on its heel.
The palest maiden of the darkest hair of brown
And languid eyes of temptation to surely drown
The weakest hearts, arose from the swift fallen wreckage
From hidden and surfacing roots that tipped her carriage.
Yet with the shock, a faint ensued and maiden fell.
She was under care, yet they were under her spell.

Her name was Carmilla and though she seemed as sweet
As kisses from the sun, to pry lips was a feat.
Her words were murmured like soft lullabies above
And such entrapments made fools oft fall for her love.
Yet her most silent secrets were more shrouded than
The whispers of the moon's eventide waning span.
Before the maid became a new guest, a nightmare
Emerged from memory in which she did ensnare
The senses of fair Laura, lady of the schloss.
Yet that could not be and she would not be so cross.

The moon, this night, is full of such odylic charm
So how could its silvery splendor observe harm?
Decay and death ensued across the nearby town
Yet death brought not a crease to Carmilla's fair crown.
Her strange disappearances, she assured, were walks
From sleep yet she could not explain the secure locks.
A weakness grew from needle pricks in Laura's breast
And a suspicion lurked and hinted to their guest....

Accompanied by a true friend, the lord and Laura
Abruptly trekked toward the plains of stone and flora.
The very last of countesses would have been buried
In tombs beneath the chapel where they were once carried.
The Ruins of Karnstein, where rumored, lay fine Mircalla.
The countess, sly as snakes and swift as the impala,
Did lay as if asleep and realization struck.
It was she! Our guest lay in dull marble and muck!
The axe was raised and her scream issued, filled with dread.
The axe then fell and she was silenced, she was dead.

--After Sheridan Le Fanu's *Carmilla*

CHATTERBOX
Phil Hickes

Phil Hickes is English and lives in Portland, Oregon with his wife who he met while living in New Zealand. They also have a rescue dog called Lucky who's prone to bouts of melancholy when separated from his ball. Hickes loves Autumn, stone circles and crumbling English graveyards. He's had a number of shorts published and is currently subbing his second book, a middle grade horror yarn. You can follow him on Twitter if so inclined @hickesy.

THE MURMUR OF CONVERSATION from her father's study told Greer it was just past two o'clock. She didn't need to inspect the golden carriage clock on the dining room mantelpiece to know this. The sounds of her father's daily routine were more accurate than anything laboured over by myopic Swiss craftsmen. The kettle's shrill whistle prised her eyes open at exactly twenty past seven every morning. The surly grumble of their antiquated heating system being shut down informed her that it was just past ten o'clock at night: time to lay her leather bookmark on the page and pretend to be asleep before her father came in to kiss her goodnight. Greer had learned to structure her own movements according to his audible routine.

Now it was two o'clock: the time he put aside to talk business on the telephone. She pressed her ear to the door.

"Oh, I am sorry to hear...yes...yes...that would be fine..."

He would remain in his study until four o'clock, before emerging to prepare them both a light tea. Then he would go in to see to his clients. It meant she had two hours, which was more than enough. Listening for a few more seconds to ensure he really was deep in conversation, she wandered down towards the waiting room to see who was there.

With a thriving practice in the town, the two of them were rarely alone in their large Victorian house. She appreciated that her father must be good at his job, because people were willing to wait a long time to be granted time alone with him, though she didn't know why they just didn't arrive a little later. It wasn't as if her father ever changed his routine. The upside of this was that most afternoons, there would always be someone for her to talk to. It was the highlight of her day, which were invariably dull and uneventful. She didn't go to school anymore.

In a way, Greer considered making polite conversation her own small contribution. Alleviating people's boredom while they waited for her father was good for business. Not that it was an inconvenience. Unlike many nine-years-olds, she didn't suffer from shyness in front of her father's acquaintances. Her tongue was never tied and she enjoyed learning about the many different lives being led outside of their front door. Truth be told, she considered her afternoon conversations more educational than her morning lessons.

She paused to straighten her braids and pick a thread of cotton from her dress. Twirling it between her fingers, she dropped on the floor, watching it spiral down like a sycamore seed. A smart appearance was essential in a business environment. People were more inclined to take you seriously. She'd learned that from her father. Clearing her throat with a soft cough, she twisted the brass doorknob and peered around the door.

Sometimes it would be quite busy, but today there was only one person waiting. A man with silver hair stood with his arms clasped behind his back, staring intently at the portrait her father kept on the wall. Greer had stared at it herself, many times. It depicted storm clouds hovering low over a wintry landscape. The eye of the observer was drawn by a shaft of sunlight, which had broken free of the caliginous canopy to shine down on the mountains below.

Greer waited. Sometimes the customers didn't like to talk and would ignore her until she left. Some people were obviously unnerved by her presence. But on this occasion, sensing her scrutiny, the man turned. He was old, with a face like an unmade bed, all wrinkled and creased. He smiled at her with a look of mild surprise on his face. Greer found herself smiling back. She imagined many people before her had done the same.

"Hello there. Are you the receptionist?" he said. His voice sounded a little croaky, as though he needed a sip of water.

Greer felt her cheeks warm. It felt good to be addressed in such professional tones, even though she appreciated that the man was just being kind.

"No, I'm Mister Rowe's daughter, Greer," she replied. "My father won't be available for another couple of hours."

"Oh, I see. Well, I suppose I'll just keep waiting if that's okay. I don't have much else to do. Rather in here than outside in that horrible storm."

The rain had been clawing at the windows all day. Greer was glad to be inside, too. Whilst the heating system complained at regular intervals, it was good at its job and kept the icy winter temperatures at bay. Besides, she didn't like going outside, even when it was sunny. It was too big.

The man stepped forward and stretched out his hand.

"Arthur. Pleasure to meet you."

Greer took his hand and shook it three times. That seemed appropriate. His hand was cold, but then it was the middle of winter. Cold hands, warm heart, she thought.

"Nice to meet you, Arthur," she replied.

The man smiled again and gestured to the painting.

"I was just admiring your picture. Very...transcendental."

"Yes," Greer said. She wasn't wholly sure what *transcendental* meant and so remained silent. The man smiled again and looked down at the floor, then back at the painting, seemingly unsure of where the next conversational stepping stone lay. After a few seconds, the man sighed and spoke again.

"Is your father always this busy? I seem to have been here a long time." He tapped his watch. "Though I'm unsure exactly *when* I arrived. My watch seems to have stopped, stupid thing."

"Yes, I'm afraid he is. Always busy."

As the man didn't appear to mind her presence, Greer felt comfortable enough to ask him a question of her own. There were those that liked to talk and there were those that didn't. He seemed like the former. In her experience, one or two questions were all it took to spark up an engaging dialogue.

"What do you do, Arthur?" she asked.

The man raised his white eyebrows.

"Oh, not a lot these days. I used to be in the building trade. Ran my own business. Had to retire early due to ill health, but thankfully I'd made enough money by then. I wouldn't recommend it. Not that you're probably looking to become a bricklayer - are you?"

Greer giggled and shook her head. She wanted to take over the business from her father. Talking to the customers was her passion.

Greer gestured towards a chair.

"Why don't you sit down, Arthur? My father's going to be a while yet."

"Thank-you, I do feel a bit tired today," the man said, coming to sit down beside her. As if to emphasise his weariness, he broke off into a violent coughing fit. Greer waited patiently until he was finished, noticing that he turned his head away from her to spit something into his handkerchief, which he quickly screwed up and slipped in his pocket before she had chance to have a good look. She didn't mind. She'd seen far worse. All her father's clients were in a bad way. That was why they came. Noticing he was being observed, the man banged his fist against his chest, as if berating the guilty culprit.

"Sorry about that, can't seem to shake this chest cold."

"It's alright, that's why you're here, isn't it?"

The man's baggy eyes narrowed as he stared off into the distance.

"Yes, I suppose it is."

"Don't worry, my father will be able to help."

They fell silent again. The old man stared out of the window. Not willing to relinquish the conversation just yet, Greer sat down beside him and touched him on the arm.

"Do you have any children?"

"Eh? Oh, no love. Never seemed to find the time. Another good reason not to open your own business."

"But you have a wife?"

"Arthur's face crumpled a little. Greer knew the answer before he spoke.

"I do, yes, though I'm afraid she passed on some years ago."

"Oh. I'm sorry."

"That's okay, young lady, I'm afraid it happens to us all."

They lapsed into silence once more. Greer waited. She kicked her legs to and fro. She sighed, quite loudly. She drummed her fingers on the side of the plastic chair. But the old man didn't take her hint and continued watching the raindrops, which careered down the window in a blind panic to reach the bottom. It was okay. She'd had a little chat. That would have to do. She would leave him to wait. He obviously had a lot on his mind.

"I have to go now. Nice to meet you, Arthur. My father shouldn't be too long now."

The old man turned and smiled weakly, before raising one hand in farewell. He appeared to have run out of steam. Greer smiled once more and raised her own hand, before tiptoeing out of the waiting room and closing the door with the lightest of touches. Her father didn't know she came in here, and she didn't want him to. He'd told her not to, but that didn't matter. What he didn't know wouldn't hurt him.

Later, she sat down with her father for tea and sandwiches. He sat at the head of the dining room table. Greer sat to one side, so she didn't have to meet his gaze every time she looked up.

Their meals were taken in silence. But this afternoon, Greer noticed him glance up from his newspaper and frown. She angled her head towards the window, pretending to be interested in the swirling bands of rain that hurled themselves against the glass, like an army trying to find a breach.

"Greer, I've been thinking..."

Greer's stomach cramped. Her face flushed. Immediately she locked her eyes onto her plate. A half eaten tuna and cucumber sandwich refused to intervene, despite her silent entreaties.

"...I bumped into a friend of mine the other day," her father continued.

She could just see the glint of his spectacles out of the corner of her eye as he peered down at her. "A nice chap, Doctor Benzai. He specialises in...well, he specialises in talking to children, Greer, and I thought you might want to meet him. He might be able to help you come out of your shell a little. We can't go on like this forever you know."

Greer fought to control her breaths, which had formed an angry queue in her chest. She widened her eyes. Maybe if she could hold them open 30 seconds without blinking he'd stop.

Shut up. Shut up. Shut up. Shut up.

Her father stirred his tea. The clink of the spoon had a discordant ring, like the jangle of prison keys.

"Well, I just want you to think about it. There's no harm in a little chat."

As her father gathered the plates and rose, Greer remained still until he'd left the room. Then, keeping her eyes on the floor, and her arms by her side, she walked out and up the stairs to her bedroom.

She was safe again.

Outside, the streetlamps flickered as they began another nightshift, lending a faint orange blush to the wet pavements. She watched out of the window. Gradually, the greys darkened until the day fell away like a retreating tide.

Movement caught her eye.

The old man she'd met earlier - Arthur - was walking slowly away from their front door. She banged on the window with the palm of her hand, but only managed a muffled thud, which was quickly swallowed up the pitter-patter of the rain. An elderly lady waited for him at the end of the path, huddled inside an umbrella. As Arthur stepped through the gate, they embraced, clinging to each other with an intensity that Greer found hard to watch. She turned away, suddenly feeling like a snooper.

She hoped he felt a little better.

At some point in the night, Greer was awoken by the sound of the telephone. She heard her father clump his way downstairs. She eased herself out of the covers and crept along the landing to listen. His deep voice echoed through the house.

"Oh dear, how awful...yes of course...I'll see to it right away...no, don't worry, I wasn't asleep. That's the nature of the job I'm afraid. Okay, I'll see you tomorrow."

Greer scuttled back to her bedroom, holding her breath as she heard her father climb the stairs. She wondered what had happened. They often received phone calls at late hours, and it was normally the precursor to a busy day in the practice. Greer burrowed down beneath the sheets and wriggled her toes excitedly. Tomorrow there would be people to meet and conversations to be had. Those were always the best days.

Next morning's lesson couldn't finish fast enough. Greer sat in the dining room, hunched over her textbook. She was supposed to be reading about the English Civil War, but had decided to draw a picture of Arthur instead. In her sketch, he was building a brick wall with a big smile on his face.

At two o'clock, her father retreated to his study and Greer made her way down to the waiting room. She felt a little giddy as she pushed open the door. She never knew who would be waiting.

A mother sat with a young boy beside her. Greer knew he was her son because of the physical resemblance. They both had black hair and large noses, although the boy was missing his lower jaw so she couldn't see if they had the same mouths, too.

"Hello," Greer said.

The lady was crying and hurriedly wiped her nose, before looking up at Greer with red-rimmed eyes. The small boy tried to speak but could only manage a horrible bubbling sound, as though gargling some viscous liquid.

"Have you been here long?" Greer asked.

"I...I'm not sure," the lady said. "I can't really remember."

"Oh," Greer said. That's okay."

The small boy was poking his finger into the ragged cavity that used to be his chin.

"Stop that, Michael," his mother said. "You'll only make it worse."

"My father will be able to help with that," Greer said. "A man came in a few weeks ago that had shot himself in the head. He was very unhappy, you see, because his girlfriend had left him for another man. He told me so. Anyway, he had a huge chunk of his skull missing, but after my father had seen to him you would hardly know."

The lady didn't seem impressed. Greer was a little disappointed. She waited for the lady to compose herself. Many of her father's clients were upset when they came in. Some were confused and rambling. Others would just remain silent. Not all of them knew they were dead. Arthur had known, she'd seen it in his eyes.

"What happened to you?" Greer said. "Can you remember?"

The lady sniffled.

"No, not really. We might have been in the car. Bringing Michael home from school, that was probably it. Where are we? Who are you?"

"I'm Greer. You're at Rowe's Funeral Parlour. We're the best in town, you're lucky they didn't send you to Langham's."

"Funeral Parlour?" the lady said. Her son had kneeled up on the chair to stare out of the window.

"Yes. You've had an accident. I think that was what my father was speaking on the phone about last night."

"Oh God, has someone died?"

Greer grimaced. She thought the lady understood, particularly considering the boy's injuries. She considered elucidating, but checked herself. They had to come to that knowledge themselves. Her job was simply to comfort them.

"You don't have to worry about that right now. Just try and relax and my father will be in soon to help you."

The lady nodded, and began to rearrange her clothes, which were stiff with dun patches of congealed blood.

They fell into a long conversation. The lady, whose name was Rebecca, had worked for the council in the Planning Department, but hadn't enjoyed her job. Michael, her son, was her only child, but she'd been trying to have another before the accident happened. Her husband was called David, but she didn't know what had happened to him. She couldn't recall him being in the car. Michael calmed down after a while, too, and stared at Greer while she spoke. Every so often, his mother would pat him on the back as he struggled to clear his throat. It was one of the most enjoyable conversations Greer had had for some time, so much so that she lost track of time, and failed to notice the daylight fading. By the time she heard her father's footsteps it was too late to hide.

"Greer, what the hell are you doing!"

Greer whirled around to see her father's shocked face, the lens of his glasses catching the fading light, erasing his eyes. She pursed her mouth and burrowed her chin into her chest. She was in trouble now, and cursed inwardly - how could she have been so careless? As her father ushered her out, she caught a final glimpse of the two polished silver caskets lying on her father's preparation table, the smell of formaldehyde and methanol hanging heavy in the air, as it always did. Michael sat up in his casket and waved to her, but she couldn't wave back because her father had pinned her arms to her side, his face flushed with blood.

"Oh, Greer, you poor child."

Her father brought her back into the dining room and hugged her fiercely. A tear rolled out from beneath his spectacles. Greer had never seen him so upset before.

"I shouldn't have been so careless. Oh, Greer, you must have been terrified. I'll never forgive myself."

Greer was sorry, too. No good was going to come of this. If she were to be barred from going into the waiting room again, who would she talk to?

She dreaded to think.

***

Doctor Benzai fixed his chestnut eyes on Greer and took a deep breath. She caught a whiff of his milky breath, as though he'...d been eating porridge or something. Slowly, she turned her head away. Not that it would deter him. He was so persistent, like a piece of chewing gum on the sole of her shoe. Her father had sent her to him because he believed she was ill and needed to get better. All it had done so far was drive her mad.

"How are you feeling today, Greer? Is there anything you'd like to talk about?"

Greer stared past his shoulder. The window blinds needed cleaning.

"Yesterday we looked at some pictures, do you remember? Do you remember how they made you feel?"

Greer did remember. They'd made her feel bored. Bored to death. Same as the previous day. And the day before that.

"Don't worry, he'll get tired soon."

Greer smirked at the pale young man with the sliced wrists, who had come to sit beside Doctor Benzai. He used to live in her room.

"And when he does, you and me can sit down and have a proper chat," the young man said, winking.

Greer folded her hands in her lap and smiled.

"That would be just perfect."

TO ROT
Mariah Huehner

New York Times Best-selling writer and Harvey award nominated editor of comics and graphic novels. Titles include: *True Blood: All Together Now* , Anne Rice's *Servant of the Bones* , *RISE* for *The Witching Hour* anthology and *Emily & The Strangers*. You can find her tweeting too much as Tiredfairy.

Mariah loves cephalopods, monster girls, stories and being a mominator.

The stones wait, forgotten amongst weeds and brambles and drifts of dry, cracked leaves, as snow gently falls, blanketing over them in a hushed hiss. The names carved into them have all worn away, only the traces of dates and symbols remain. A single half skull sits in the midst of their uneven ring, browned and cracked, dug up by some animal and left to rot in the open air. Its eye sockets look up to the bright gray sky with hollow silence.

The snow falls all day and covers the small, neglected cemetery in shimmering white. It continues to wait for night to come as the snow slows, then stops. The light fades into a peachy, golden, afternoon. It glints off rooftops in the slight distance, a village or town that has forgotten the others that used to live there. The sun sets a dull red.

Darkness sets the snow aglow in the light of a half moon, cold and blue and beautiful. It falls on her face, a soft gray translucency, against the starry sky. She walks over the ground without steps, the dark strings of her hair streaming in the brittle, bitter wind.

She passes through the stones, long fingers sweeping against their tops, recalling names that no longer matter to anyone else, including her own. They help her remember and stay rooted to this world instead of the next. She is not ready to leave yet and has not been since the fire and all that came after.

Her eyes, deep pits of shadow, show just a pinprick of light at their centers, blinking and fading, like slowly dying stars, stare past everything and pierce the nothing beyond. Her mouth, wide and thin, is frozen in a cracked and unforgiving frown. She is empty now, so empty, a pit of gaping, aching, craving, need.

There is only one stone she stops for, one stone she sits by, one stone she touches with a longing, soft, sigh. It is a small stone, a little cross that lists slightly to one side. She hums to it and weeps for it and watches it as the hours while by.

Then she hears the cry.

That pale gray head turns at the sharp, wailing, sound of it, piercing across the snow covered clearing beyond the graveyard. She knows that cry. It wraps itself around her heart and she is moving towards it, fast, a blurred shadow among shadows.

She is remembering that cry from before, a hungry sound, a plaintive sound, full of desperate longing.

In the clearing, set in the middle of a different kind of stone ring from the monuments she left behind, is a small bundle. The cry from it is growing weaker, sadder, as though it knows that no one is coming for it. She looks down from her grayness and sees a small, pale, scrunched, face, with lips turning a faint blue. Tears have frozen to its cheeks as the mouth lets out ragged, hiccupping sobs.

"Shhhhhh." She says to it, her voice cracked from disuse. "Shhhhhh."

The child stops crying and looks up and smiles. It reaches two arms up to the gray figure who stoops and lifts it into her transparent arms. She looks into the child's eyes, blurry with tears, as it sticks a chubby hand into its mouth for comfort. It sucks on its fingers listlessly, eyelids drooping, it's wracking breaths slowing to ragged, shallow ones.

She coos to the child, whispers soothing nonsense and nothings. She knows it is a girl child, sickly, so small and pale for her age. It is cold in her arms but she does not feel it. She only feels the weight of it, the little limbs grasping at her, the round head pressing against her arm that is not, technically, there.

She takes it away from the fairy circle, back to the dead forgotten stones, to the place where her own daughter is buried. She sits in the middle of the faded monuments and rocks the baby whose eyes drift closed. She sings it a lullabye and touches its icy, round cheek. It makes a soft rattling sound in its throat and goes still.

When its eyes open again they are dark like her eyes, with tiny pinpoints of light deep within. It looks at her with knowing now, and smiles with tiny, sharp, glittering teeth. It is gray like her, empty like her, and it is hungry.

She smiles and takes it towards the village in the distance, the village it came from, the village that left it to die and rot, alone, among the stones.

She takes it to feed.

CARLYLE
B.C.G. Jones

B. C. G. Jones, born in the Great White North, lives in Providence, Rhode Island and works in the romantic and fast-paced world of office administrative support. A member of a very cool and helpful writer's critique group, he reads when he's awake. He's a big fan of dogs and a fan of big dogs and if he met yours they could be second-best friends (don't worry.)

No hotel has a functional speaking tube anymore, so it was a thrill to see one. That was during my re-interview at the Bastion Hotel.

Gone was the colorless clerk from my initial interview, and in his place behind the business office's desk was a sunburnt man with matted hair, filthy clothes, but with fingernails scrubbed clean.

"Roy Klosky?" he asked. I nodded and he directed me to shut the door and sit in a swivel chair. "Very excited to meet you in person. Overall this," he held up my résumé, "is just more of the same twaddle I've seen a thousand times. Good grades, experience in customer service, these are cheap, common claims. But your paid internship at Eurich Brothers Funeral Home has caught my eye."

"Yes sir. My responsibilities included inventory, cleaning the hearses..."

"I've read your curriculum vitae," he snapped. "I also know you turned down a full-time position they offered, had only glowing things to say about you. Why not take them up on it? And I'll know if you're lying, so don't."

He surprised me here. After a moment I said, "There's a dishonesty at the heart of the funeral business. People want to know their loved ones are in a better place, Heaven I guess. But we don't know, we deal only with the bodies. So we tell them what they want to hear. I don't like lying about important subjects like that."

His pen crossed his lips. "Concern with truth. My gut feeling about you was right. Come with me, Roy."

Muscles rippled under his shabby clothes. I followed him on a brisk tour of the Bastion, from the checkerboard-tile kitchen to the skylit indoor pool. With its copious arches and wrought iron, the hotel appeared as a Victorian relic modernized just enough for 21st-century use.

We came to the front desk, a carved oak structure holding vases filled with chrysanthemums and white roses.

"Discretion is key," he said. "Take this job and you'll have secrets even from most of your coworkers."

"I'm reticent by nature," I assured him. Just then something on the thick brass ring mounted on the wall caught my eye.

"That looks familiar," I said.

"That is a speaking tube. It will keep you in contact with room 307. Some of our most special guests stay there."

Speaking tube. "Oh yes," I said. "I saw one of those on a tour of the Lincoln-Tallman house out in Wisconsin. A lot of fancy houses had them during the nineteenth century. That when this one was installed?"

"Not quite," he grinned. "You see, this place was built in the early 1970s, when the Vietnam War was winding down. My father hired an architect to make it look Victorian, per his tastes. Good for me because it meant the speaking tube wouldn't be conspicuous."

"Nifty. So this room you're talking about must have a phone too."

He shook his head. "Phones won't work. Not land lines or cellular. These guests cause too much interference. Would you like to know why?"

I nodded again.

"Good. Then come work for me."

***

By the following June I was accustomed to the ways of the hotel.

The Bastion had a rooftop observatory, one of the best views in Boston, I thought. One morning I went up for a gander before my shift began. Sipping coffee, I saw the orange in the sky left over from the sunrise reflecting in the rippling waters of the Charles, the petals falling from the cherry trees and floating on the wind as if possessed, the gondoliers shaking the blossoms from their straw hats. A bride and groom tramped along the Esplanade, following their wedding photographer like obedient puppies.

I gazed on all this without much concern until I realized I wasn't alone. Whoever was with me I couldn't see, but I could feel their presence. It could only be one of the guests from 307. The guest watched me watching the scene below and I didn't know what they were thinking. The hair on the back of my neck bristled and I no longer felt secure at the roof's edge, so I went in.

At the front, Kate, the other desk clerk on duty, brushed a strand of chestnut hair out of her eyes.

"Good morning, sunshine," she said. "How's it look up there?"

"Nice," I said. "Weird. Who's the guest in 307?"

Her face grew more serious. "Carlyle's the name, Mr. Carlyle."

"Carlyle" wasn't his real name. It wasn't what he'd been called in life and I doubted anyone called him that in the afterlife. As McCulloch had alluded before, the fact that we let 307 out to specters, revenants, whatever you wanted to call them wasn't common knowledge. The desk clerks knew, some room service workers, a few housekeepers: enough to have at least one on each shift. To keep the arrangement confidential we spoke in code and referred to them by aliases, derived from transcendental and romantic thinkers.

"I think I just met him."

"Oh?" She looked at me with reluctant curiosity. The 307 guests could go anywhere except the rooms of other guests, so it was possible to meet them, but it rarely happened. I shrugged, not knowing anything well enough yet to really say. The phone rang and she answered, taking somebody's reservation for Labor Day weekend.

Clarence, a big young man with tidy yellow hair, pushed his room service delivery cart past us. A wheel hit a snag in the faux Persian carpet and a tray on the top went flying, stainless steel dish cover first. Food fell on the floor: broken eggshells crusted in dry yolk, moldy toast with curdled butter, mangled jelly packets. It had to be going to room 307. The spirits of the dead subsist on dead food. He cursed and cleaned up.

Clarence was in the know. He'd grown up tagging through the South in his mother's psychic medicine show. She was mostly a fraud, but not completely.

"Boss man's dropping in," he said after Kate hung up. "Don't know why but word is he's driving down from Vermont."

McCulloch lived in a monastery outside Rutland for much of the year. I never knew what order, or broadly speaking what religion they were part of. Men with dark suits and shaven heads, some had visited the hotel but spoken to no one. Rumors abounded about the things they taught him, including how to raise demons and change eye color. But there was also a rumor that McCulloch had eaten his twin in utero, so it was hard to know what to believe.

"It'll be nice to see him again," Kate said without commitment as Clarence wheeled away.

The whistle on the speaking tube sounded, and since I was closest I answered it. I heard the pause before I heard the voice. The silence was the most important part of the speech.

"Hello. Is this the service coordinator?"

"You can call us that. This is Mr. Carlyle I presume?"

"Yes. Yes, I am. I must request something." Words measured, like Ikea components he wasn't sure where to put.

"We're here to help, sir."

"A long wooden box lies on the floor here, a heart carved on the front. It clutters, I dislike it and want it gone."

Ah, Mrs. Fuller, the previous guest. She'd asked for a hope chest. We didn't know why, or if she'd been married. Questions like that we didn't ask.

"I'll have the man bringing you your breakfast help me. We'll get rid of it right away."

"Good. Move nothing else."

I told Kate to hold down the fort. She flashed a thumbs up as a pair of newlywed soldiers stepped forward to check in.

Clarence and his cart almost ran me over when I got up there. He'd made his delivery and was coming back down.

"Hold up, Clar," I said. "Guest wants us to get rid of Fuller's glory box."

"That monstrosity? Carlyle's got some taste after all. You can go now. I'll handle it myself."

"Don't be an idiot. We don't need you slipping a vertebra."

He stowed the cart and I swiped the keycard. Carlyle gave us no sign if he was there. The hope chest lay between the two beds. As Clarence and I prepared to lift it I glanced over at the vanity.

"Hold on a sec," I said and went over for a better look. Six photographs lay before the mirror. Family portraits, they showed a man and woman and their son. As they progressed more of the son was scratched out.

Clarence and I returned to business, hoisting the chest away. Once we were downstairs we went out back and tossed it in the dumpster.

"You see those pictures?" I asked.

"Probably just working some stuff out," Clarence said. "Ghosts do that sometimes."

Back at the desk, Kate smiled and placated a woman complaining that she hadn't gotten a wakeup call. She hadn't asked for one, but nothing is ever some people's fault. Kate had a brief career as an EMT, so she was good under pressure. For my part I checked in a British family decked out in touristy Boston gear, the reserved mother wearing a t-shirt that read "Wicked Smaht."

"Just saw McCulloch's car," Kate said when everyone had gone. His car was hard to miss, a black Saab ragtop with bright silver upholstery.

He strode in a minute later, tanned and hale in a seersucker suit. The crowd parted before him and fell silent, but one woman in a yellow sundress approached him.

"Excuse me, sir," she said. "When you first came in I could have sworn

53

there was a halo around your head."

Head back, laughing, he said, "The brothers I've been staying with have kept me busy in the fields. Maybe that's scored me some angel points."

She giggled and fell back into her group. He came toward us and leaned forward on the desk.

"Mr. Klosky. Ms. Rose. It's occurred to me that I've been a selfish man."

"How's that?" Kate asked.

"Our guests in room 307 are such fascinating, vibrant people, and they've told me so much. Yet I've been monopolizing them. Even my most valuable employees have only had fleeting contact with these worthies." He handed us each an invitation on cardstock. "Well, no more. Mr. Carlyle has been such a joy to talk to, and I want to share the experience. We're having a get-together tonight. Attendance is optional, but it would mean a lot to me."

"Carlyle?" I said. "Really?"

McCulloch and Kate both gave me looks. "Yes, of course," McCulloch said. "Why not?"

"He just seems a little off to me. A little uncomfortable. No offense."

"None taken. But you must understand, some of our friends have been away a long time. They've been out of the habit of normal social intercourse, and their edges may have grown rough again. So it may be with Mr. Carlyle. If this makes you want to avoid him…"

"No, no, I'll be there. If he's your friend he can't be all bad."

McCulloch smiled, clapped me on the shoulder, and asked after Clarence's whereabouts.

***

After a catnap and a lukewarm shower at home I returned to the Bastion and scanned the lobby for anyone I might know. When I'd given up and started toward the stairwell, Kate snuck up behind me and said "boo." Ghosts don't do this. I laughed despite the tameness of the joke and we walked up together.

It must be said that room 307 was pretty spacious. All the employees who knew about the kind of guests who stayed there could have fit in comfortably, as McCulloch had planned. As it was so far the number reached ten when Kate and I walked in. In the center was McCulloch, calling out, "Don't be shy, people. Dig in." Indeed a good amount of food was on hand, including crudités, barbecue chicken wings, and yes, champagne.

Clarence had come with his sister Sally. When I waved Clarence gave me a brief nod and Sally pretty much ignored me in favor of another guy from

54

room service, a situation that seemed to have Clarence concerned.

I knelt in front of the vanity and looked in the mirror to make sure I hadn't missed a spot shaving or anything. The scarred photos were gone, removed by someone or other. Anyway, I looked decent enough as these things go, but the background was off. I could see the other attendees, the king size beds and wing back chairs, but the view had too much space. The room as reflected seemed to go on forever. I stood back and felt the room spinning. McCulloch caught me before I could fall.

Speaking to everyone, he said, "I must ask you all to keep back from the vanity. I'll be needing it to contact Mr. Carlyle in a few minutes."

For the next few minutes his eye darted between the guests who'd arrived and the still open door, where he seemed to hope more would come. Finally he gave up, closed the door, and sat down in front of the mirror. He tapped his champagne flute to quiet the rest of us down. We settled in comfortable spots and watched hm.

McCulloch pressed his hands together as in prayer and stared into the glass, a vein throbbing in his temple. Minutes passed that I wasn't timing. When it seemed like nothing might happen, the reflection smiled at him. McCulloch himself wasn't smiling, and this gave him a visible jolt.

"Carlyle?"

"Yes, my friend, it is good to talk to you again," the man in the mirror said.

"Likewise, but why…"

"Why am I wearing your face? A whim, nothing more. We disembodied spirits must entertain ourselves how we can."

"Well then by all means. I've brought some other friends of mine and I'd like them to know what you can tell us of what you've learned, what the afterlife is like."

"Bleak," Carlyle said. "Unremittingly bleak and featureless. I see movement sometimes, shapes in the distant fog. Almost always turns out to be nothing."

McCulloch's brows knit. "Strange, that doesn't square with what I've heard before."

Empty-eyed, Carlyle said, "Afterlife is informed by one's life proper, and I didn't have much."

McCulloch shook his head, not comprehending.

"I'll clarify," Carlyle said. "Sometime in the womb I became conscious. I knew, or thought I knew, that I was safe, protected. And I saw, inches away, another boy, my brother, my friend. Again, so I thought.

"How little I knew. I didn't imagine this other boy would attack me, absorb what little flesh I had."

McCulloch grimaced. "Attacked? You make it sound like there was malice on your twin's part. To me it sounds like he was just surviving. No sinister plan involved."

"Perhaps. At any rate I'm not angry, not anymore. I've made my peace. But I am curious about you, Mr. McCulloch, and your singular life. Your business, travels, your lovers." Staring out from the mirror, he took stock of the group. "I grow bashful, though, and I'm sure our conversation would bore the others."

McCulloch stood, turned, took a small bow. "He's right. You may as well go home and rest. I can comp cab rides for those who need them."

So it looked like the party was over. Out in the hall I drifted back to the people I knew best, Kate and Clarence. Sally had already left with the other guy, which Kate was consoling Clarence about.

"She's young, man. We girls need to make our mistakes."

He nodded and said something about how he'd been raising her for years. Before I could join in a noise from the room broke my concentration, the double thump of a chair and body hitting the floor. The door was just barely ajar and I ran in to find McCulloch sprawled out on the floral carpet.

"What's going on?" Clarence asked from the doorway. "Is he..?"

I lowered my ear to McCulloch's face. "Don't hear him breathing," I said.

Kate pushed her way past Clarence and nudged me out of the way as well. "Let me do this." She performed CPR on him, chest compressions first, then mouth-to-mouth. She looked doubtful and discouraged, shaking her head. Just then McCulloch stirred and his eyes opened. Clarence charged forward to help him up.

"Sir, are you okay?"

McCulloch rose on shaky legs that he steadied apparently through force of will. He looked around the room, at the three of us.

"I'm alive," he said. "Yes, this is life. And I'm going to live it. There's so much for me to do out there."

In the mirror I saw a twinkle. No, I saw McCulloch's face pressed up against the glass, his hands clutching for an escape. Or was it Carlyle? That seemed to make more sense. But as I approached the vanity the reflection faded and I only saw myself. A strong hand grabbed my shoulder.

"That's enough of that," McCulloch said. "Don't worry about the mirror now. The mirror's fine, and so is the man in it. Go home."

DEAD AND BREAKFAST
K. Trap Jones

K. Trap Jones is an author of horror novels and short stories. With inspiration from Dante Alighieri and Edgar Allan Poe, he has a temptation towards narrative folklore, classic literary works and obscure segments within society. His short stories have appeared in various anthologies and magazines. His novel, *The Sinner* won the 2010 Royal Palm Literary Award. Other novels include: *The Drunken Exorcist, The Charm Hunter, The Harvester, One Bad Fur Day* and *The King's Ox.*

He is also a member of the Horror Writers Association and can be found lurking around Tampa, FL. For more information visit: http://ktrapjones.wordpress.com.

I don't consider what I had to do a burden; more like a chore. I may not like or agree with the responsibility which had been placed upon me, but nevertheless, the task had to be completed. During my tenure, I tried to run an honest business; a bed and breakfast where the customers could feel at home. My staff had pride in making sure each of the customer's needs was met with the utmost attention. It was the theory behind the tradition in which had kept us afloat long before my time. An ideology; an understanding of how things must operate in order to prosper. There are plenty of other establishments to choose from, but I believed it was the warmth and unrelenting hospitality which made us stand out from the rest.

To be different was something most tried desperately to achieve, but we never had to worry about that. We thrived on dead memories; the knowledge and mindset which the recently deceased emit when they first pass over. It is both a gift and a curse. Each one of us had a purpose; a singular function which kept the place running on course, but like everything else, it too is limited. Time was the enemy of the recently deceased. Every second ticking by was one step closer to leaving. A purgatory of sorts; built into the law of the death process in which time was granted.

The period of time, a pause between the living world and the afterlife, was often misunderstood and wasted within brutal states of confusion and duress. Dying is not easy; it is a tormented onslaught on the human mind. Complete destruction of the thought process takes place when the body ceases to function, but it is the separation between body and mind which generates the new relationship with death. However, the process is not without its flaws. Much like the living world, bargains can be achieved; both good and evil can influence those in their most weakened states. It was within one of the pauses in the process where I found myself. A demented cycle of torturous repetitiveness; so vile even the devil himself couldn't dream of it.

Long before my time, a curse was placed on the property. A rogue witch from the darkest bayous of the south stood trial upon the very land. Death by fire was the scorned sentence of justice. Legends speak of her forked tongue lavishing the flames; sparking an eternal curse hell bent with black magic and voodoo hatred towards the accusers. Her peers, the ones who cast her to death, exhaled their final breaths as she did. The entrapped souls bled the land, destroying every morsel of life that dared to tread upon the tainted soil. As the law of death continued, more souls were needed to replace the forsaken whose time had reached the end. A replacement pattern began to take place; a cleansing of the land in order to rejuvenate the curse so it could continue. Each abandoned soul was burdened to find a replacement so the chores of the dead would be tended to.

Many years later, an unknowing entrepreneur took a liking to the cheap, undeveloped land and erected the bed and breakfast, *The Manor*. The entrapped, bored souls took a liking to the manor and came to the understanding that the living would come to them during their time of need. Finding replacements became easy; they could even be picky. They all feared the demented afterlife of failure if they did not find a replacement by the time they left the living land. Soon, the entire staff of the newly created bed and breakfast was dead. Through freak accidents and timely mishaps, the staff began a newly established process in which they would continue to work until their time ran out. Prior to that, they must find a replacement for their particular job and worthy of the task to keep the establishment running successfully.

I visited the bed and breakfast with my wife during a summer vacation. The landscape was breathtaking and provided a much needed stress free couple of days. I remember everything about the day I died. The manager took a liking to us and made sure we had everything we needed for an excellent vacation. I thought nothing of it at the time; just perfect customer service to ensure I would return as a repeat customer. My wife and I had gotten up early to go swimming before it became too crowded. Once down by the water, we relaxed in the lawn chairs and enjoyed the breeze of the vacation.

"Excuse me, I'm terribly sorry to bother you," the manager's voiced rang out.

"Hi there," I said, trying to squint against the sun.

"I hate to disturb you, but I am in quite the bind. You see, my maintenance guy is in town getting supplies. He was fixing the light on the front porch and carelessly left an exposed wire dangling. I worry that it may spark. With my bad leg and all, I cannot climb the ladder. Could I bother you to tape up the wire for me?"

"I guess, I'm not much of a handy man, but I don't see why I can't give it a shot."

We walked through the main foyer and out the front door. Sure enough, the porch light was taken apart and an exposed wire was swinging in the wind. The porch ceiling was higher than most. The architecture of the structure created a dome which funneled further up.

"I do appreciate this. I would do it myself, but I cannot apply too much pressure on this bum leg of mine," the manager stated holding a roll of duct tape.

I'm not one for climbing ladders, especially old rickety ones like the one he carried over to me. The damn thing was about rusted closed and the grinding noise of the hinges was deafening when he pulled the ladder open.

"I'll hold the ladder for you. Here, don't forget the tape," he said, trying to stabilize the ladder.

Honestly, I didn't want to touch the ladder. It was so rusty that I felt I thought I needed a tetanus shot just to be around it. I felt the first rung crack as my foot landed upon it. None of it added to a good recipe, but the manager had a way about him. The wire was actually stressing him out and really, taping up a wire should not have been a troublesome task, but foreseeing danger was never a strong suit for me. My stomach felt uneasy with every rung I climbed. Flakes of rust fell as I gripped the ladder. I was pretty high up as I came close to the wire. The wind toyed with my balance and the creaking sounds of the ladder plagued my thoughts.

"How are you doing up there?" the manager yelled from below.

"I almost got it. I just need to tape it."

"Thank you for helping me. I was in quite a bind."

"No problem, happy to help out," I replied, removing my hands from the ladder in order to tear off a piece of tape.

I thought maybe the wind was distorting his voice as I couldn't make out his words. He kept mumbling down there, but as the wind stopped, it all became clear.

"I am forever grateful and forever sorry."

"What?" I said, briefly looking down.

I saw his hands let go of the ladder and proceeded to kick the base out. My eyes widened in confusion as the ladder became off-balanced. My feet left the rung as I dropped the tape in hopes to grasp onto something,

but nothing was there. I remember falling, looking up to the light fixture. Everything slowed down. The roll of tape was hovering next to my head and the wind was cooling my bare chest. I heard the ladder crash against the floor as the exposed wire got further away. I don't remember hitting the floor. All I saw was the manager standing over me when I opened my eyes.

"I am truly sorry, but I had to. You are a perfect replacement."

I had no voice to respond, but could feel my tongue forming words.

"It'll all come back; be patient and wait for your soul to exit."

Visions rapidly flashed before my eyes; memories, both dead and recent. The amount of anxiety was bleeding my brain; my heart felt like it was going to explode.

"Stay with me. It will all be over soon."

I couldn't feel anything; I couldn't move a muscle. Only my vision was apparent. Like a breath of air, I saw the manager's face get closer. It felt like I was standing face to face with him.

"There now, it's all done."

"I...I..."

"It's alright, your basic functions will return in due time and the essence of your body will surround your soul."

Looking down, I saw my body lying lifeless on the floor.

"We must deal with this first."

The manager went back into the foyer, yelling about an accident. My soul floated inside as I witnessed all of the staff smiling. My wife was the only one who appeared distraught as she raced to my body. Crying hysterically, she pulled my body up and held it close. I had nothing left; it all remained within my corpse. The foyer became a haven for the dead; souls were flying about through the cracks in the walls. I could only watch as the coroner zipped up my body and carried it away. I wanted to keep the vision of the body within my sight. I walked down the front steps, but could not advance any more. Both my wife and body were gone.

"The probation period is not fun; I'm sure you have a lot of questions," the manager said from behind.

"What is this?"

"It is the process of how this place functions. For the lack of a better description; it is a rinse and repeat. We cannot stay within purgatory forever; it is unjust and unacceptable, therefore we must pick our replacements when our time is up."

"Replacements?"

"When I leave, you become the new manager. Look at it as a promotion; it's easier that way."

"How long?"

"We all have different sands of time; each one is poured separately. You will never truly know until the end approaches. My time has come, the bells toll for me now. You should feel proud. After researching all of the potential candidates, you were the most qualified."

"Proud? You killed me."

"Just a formality, really. We dead are not very good at emotions. One day, you will have to make the same difficult choice. Regardless, the relief of finding a quality replacement overshadows any grief there may be. Look at your hand."

Holding my arm up, it was becoming less transparent.

"It is not tangible flesh; at least not what you are used to. You can interact with the living world and your body appearance will remain the same. Basically you are a visible ghost that appears alive. Not a bad way to go; it could be worse."

His words did not comfort me; nothing could change the fact that I was dead for doing a good deed. It made me wonder if I would still be sitting by the pool with my wife if I had just said *no*.

The manager left me within a few days after I died. Within that timeframe, he taught me everything there was to know about running the bed and breakfast. I had no choice, but to come to grips with the changes in my reality. I was dead; there was no going back so why not make the best of it. I had a great business to run and a wonderful staff under my wing that barely needed managing. Without the stress of the real world, I actually began to relax. I had no bills, no debt, and no worries. Everything was going great until death revealed itself again in the form of a customer floating face down in the pool. I stood next to the pool maintenance man as he fished the body out with a net.

"He should work out just fine, boss," he said.

The replacement process took some time to get used to as I never knew when I would see death. The staff turnover rate was unpredictable as no one truly knew when the bell would toll for them. Each one had to choose their own replacement; I could only hope that the new ones were as dependable as the last.

Years passed as I did my best to keep the business running. I became immune to the rate of death I was witnessing. I became a counselor of sorts to the newly deceased; easing their rotation into purgatory. During one session with the new receptionist, I heard the faint sound of a bell. I thought nothing of it because it was barely noticeable. The next morning it chimed again, but louder than the first. As I was showing a new maid where the break room was, I heard it again.

"Did you hear that?" I said, holding open the door.

"Hear what?" she replied.

"A bell."

"No, I didn't hear anything."

I heard it again the same night. Walking through the kitchen, I saw the chef with a client. As I watched him teaching the client to sharpen knives, I knew what he was doing.

"Can I talk to you for a second?"

"Certainly."

"You hear it, don't you?"

"The bell? Yes, that man over there has cooking experience."

"How much time do you have once you first hear?"

"I was told that it serves as a warning. You don't want it to stop. Once it does, it is too late. You've failed in her eyes. You do not want to fail."

"Her?"

"I don't know; it's just what I was told. I guess, we'll all find out. Until then, I wouldn't wait too long if you are hearing it. If you don't mind, I need to get back. Hopefully it won't be a messy one," he stated, pulling out a sharpened cleaver.

The chime was louder as I stood on the porch. My eyes grew heavy; my back ached as I stretched to get comfortable. The next chime was so loud that it actually made me jump. I knew what I had to do, but it didn't make it any easier. Although, the unknown was easily more intimidating. To find peace for my troubled mind, I walked to the study and came across a man reading a book.

"Looks like I'm not the only one having trouble sleeping," I said.

"Not much as a heavy sleeper; my eyes need to stay busy in order to get tired," he said with a smile.

"Mind if I join you?"

"You do own this place including that chair," he laughed.

"Where you from?"

"Outskirts of Tampa. I'm up here on a business trip. I don't like staying in those large, corporate hotels. Too much commotion."

"I hear you; peace and quiet is where it is at these days. At least that's what I keep telling myself. How long you staying with us for?"

"Few days. Nice place, wish it was for longer."

A sigh left my mouth as I heard another chime. His words echoed in my head as I said good night and left him. Every time I doubted whether I could handle the task or not, the bell reminded of the answer. By the morning, the loudness rattled my mind and violently brought me back to reality. Not knowing how much time was indeed left was destroying everything I was made of.

Panicking, I pushed my way through the foyer and outside onto the porch. I needed something to ease my mind; anything at all to calm my nerves.

"Great morning for a jog," a voice startled me from behind.

"Yes, yes," I replied, twisting and seeing the man dressed in running attire.

I was breathing heavy as another chime rang out. I looked up, preparing to close my eyes and find comfort. Instead, I stared directly at the porch light which was still broken. Even the wire was dangling. It was the answer I needed; it was the information I desired.

"Can I...can I ask you a favor?"

"Sure."

"The light up there, it's um...broken. The maintenance man went into town and won't be back for some time. That wire is causing me some grief. I just don't want it cause a fire."

"Oh yeah, I see it."

"Would it be too much to ask if you could tape it up? I would do it myself, but I have a bum knee."

"Hey, no problem. Do you have a ladder?"

"Yeah, I'll be right back. Let me go get one."

Toting the rusty ladder, I came back around to the porch and grinded the hinges in order to get it open. He immediately jumped up onto the first rung.

"Here's the tape. Just secure the wire so it isn't loose."

I watched as his feet kept climbing up. My hands were gripping the ladder, but I could see through the skin. I was becoming transparent and noticed the rusty ladder through my bones.

"Almost there, just need to tape it up. Yeah, this thing is definitely a hazard."

My breathing became erratic and my pulse quickened as I let go of the ladder and stepped back. My chest was disappearing and my hands no longer existed. I was running out of time as the bell chimed louder, deafening my hearing. I wanted to hold my temple to ease the pain, but I couldn't.

"I think I got it. You may have to replace the whole fixture though, it's pretty worn out."

I was vanishing at a rapid pace as I saw his foot stepped down one rung. I had to make a choice. My time was up; the bell had tolled for me. I waited too long.

"I...am..."

"What?" he said, looking down.

"I am forever grateful and forever sorry."

KNITTING AWAY ETERNITY
Christian A. Larsen

Christian A. Larsen grew up in Park Ridge, Illinois and graduated from Maine South High School in 1993. He has worked as an English teacher, radio personality, newspaper reporter, and a printer's devil. His debut novel, *Losing Touch*, features a foreword by *New York Times* bestselling-author Piers Anthony. In *Losing Touch*, Morgan Dunsmore, who is in the midst of a mid-life crisis, finds that he can walk through walls. Larsen lives with his wife and two sons in the fictional town of Northport, Illinois. Follow him on Twitter @exlibrislarsen or visitwww.exlibrislarsen.com.

Her face was sunken. That wasn't new. Her face had always been sunken, but from the outside, like the years had been chiseling grooves in her face, one line at a time. But now it was sinking from the inside. It would have been too obvious if it was cancer, too perfect. The metaphor would almost be played. But it wasn't cancer, and Laura knew it.

She had seen the slow creep of death come over other residents like a late afternoon shadow, but Dorothy was different. There were no long shadows on her. Even though she was in the shade, she cast the long shadows, sitting in the rocker near the bay window, knitting her hundredth scarf, or maybe her thousandth.

"Morning, Missus Loney," said Laura, leaning forward with both of her hands on the insides of her knees. She had seen her kindergarten teacher do that, or maybe her preschool teacher, and always thought it made a faceless pair of adult legs look so much less threatening.

Dorothy set her knitting in her lap, her bent, knobby fingers piling on top of the needles and yarn so that Laura couldn't quite make out where one ended and the other began. Crinkles of skin bunched up at her eyes. It moved when she squinted or smiled (and she looked to be doing both at the moment), but seemed so disconnected from the flesh underneath that Laura wondered if there were fishing line threaded through the high points, like Dorothy's face was a marionette—just her face—and the puppeteer was hiding in the attic.

"Morning, sweetheart," said Dorothy, reaching hard for Laura's name but not quite grabbing it. The fishing line went slack and her squinting smile faded just a touch. Her mouth creaked open just a little, an opening to a dry, toothless tunnel with no train in sight.

Dorothy Loney was supposed to have been a singer of some note back in her youth, but the details were sketchy—muddled—like a lot of residents' memories. Death wasn't the only thing that cast long shadows.

Time could do that, too. And it stretched the truth into all sorts of shapes.

"You want me to wheel you away from the window?" asked Laura, reaching for the nearest handle of the wheelchair while she watched the motes of dust slide down the shaft of sunlight like an intangible water slide. "It's gettin' on to be that time, don'tcha think?"

"S'pose so ... s'pose so," said Dorothy, nodding with her chin working its way down to her chest, making it impossible for a casual observer to tell if she was agreeing with Laura, or if she was just falling asleep.

Laura knew better, though. Having worked at Golden Oakes for almost five years, she had never known Dorothy to nod off. In fact, now that she thought about it, she had never even seen her sleeping. It was common for older folks to sleep less than other people, but she *never* saw her sleeping—not even once. Not even the time she was covering for one of the third shift nurses and stuck her head in Dorothy's room to check on the odd sound coming from inside. Her roommate was snoring so loudly it sounded like she was farting out of her nose, but Dorothy was laying still on the bed, plank straight with her bony hands folded over her middle, like a corpse in repose, except that her eyes were wide open, and the halogen lamp outside her window glinted off of them like moonlight. She went in to check her pulse, but when she reached for Dorothy's wrist, the old woman smiled with that same fish-line crinkle.

"How's this?" asked Laura, positioning the wheelchair on the other side of the window, where the light would creep away from her rather than towards her. It was also behind the TV in the common room. Dorothy never watched TV, either. Even the classics from the 40s that all the 'greatest generation' folks lapped up like cats at a saucer.

"Fine. Just fine, sweetheart," said Dorothy, picking up her knitting in her spidery hands and continuing on with the next row like she hadn't quit the last.

"You let me know if you need anything else, m'kay?" asked Laura, bent slightly at the hips and knees, her hands on her thighs like the kindergarten teacher again.

Dorothy smiled again, the bunched skin on her face almost translucent, even in the darkest corner of the room. She was the spitting image of Father Time, if he'd had a sex change before the androgyny finally set in.

Laura sat down in the office, a room that had been designed for one desk, but it now housed three, the product of the bureaucracy proliferating through incest. The window to the foyer was a mirror on the other side, slightly tinted, and the grayness reminded Laura of Ms. Loney, and how she liked things dim. She sat down at her desk and surveyed it like a Civil War general surveying the site of a future battle. *Men will die this day*, she thought.

"Hey, Laura," said Jerry, shuffle stepping around her desk to his—the one under the window. "How've things got you today?"

"By the balls, which is no mean trick," she answered. It still felt like she was getting away with something, referencing male anatomy in such a crude manner at a state-funded facility like Golden Oakes. But Jerry wasn't going to tell, and neither was Madelene, the nutritionist. She could swear like a sailor, but only when the door was closed. The main office had become a sort of confessional for them, where they dealt with beadledom of the job and the grief that poured forth when a resident that they really liked died. *Poured forth*, like the bottle of Ouzo that Laura kept in her desk for just such occasions—and head colds, another official excuse.

"I saw you wheel Dorothy to her late morning spot," said Jerry. "That was nice."

"Once a nurse, always a nurse."

"The thing I don't get is why she doesn't just start there."

"She likes the sunlight."

"Yeah, she just doesn't like it *on* her."

"Imagine ... a thing like vanity—at her age."

It was Laura's turn to talk, but a thought lodged in the Broca's area of her brain, and robbed her of language. *At her age*, Jerry had said. Jerry, who had been working at Golden Oakes for twelve years, and knew Dorothy Loney as well as any of them here in the office. As well as anyone she knew, except for Victor, the orderly who would probably still be pushing his cart at Golden Oakes until time ended. Still, he had to be in his early sixties— and Laura had seen him age in the last couple of years. The little things, like that gimp in his step, and the retreat of his silver hairline. Each month a little more of that smooth scalp skin showed a little more.

But Dorothy ... Dorothy was so old now, maybe, that you couldn't see time creeping up on her the same way, except maybe in the sinking of her face. Smiles notwithstanding, it was like the whole thing was frowning—not just her mouth.

"How old *is* Miss Loney?" Laura finally asked, staring at the paperwork on her desk, but not really seeing it. At that moment, it looked like stacks of cuneiform.

"She moved in before we digitized the files—before the fire."

That was before Laura's time. A night nurse and janitor had been rolling joints in the vault and got a little sloppy with the sparks. The fire didn't spread outside the vault, but all the records were wrecked, but that was nothing compared to the hell of evacuating all the old folks in the middle of the night. Laura was glad she missed that one. Most people missed that one. It was years ago, and reconstructing the paperwork wasn't all that bad, in retrospect. Some of the residents could do it themselves, and the ones that didn't had families—all except Dorothy.

She said she had been there since 1983, moved in from another home before that, and maybe several others. Missus Loney could be sketchy with details sometimes. Laura talked with her a lot. *Hand-patting* conversations, she called them, but the particulars were somewhat outrageous. Here it was 2014, and the sweet old lady in the wheelchair with the spaghetti plate of knitting in her lap said she was married in 1910. Married a Rambler dealer named Loney. Never had kids, and lost their fortune in the crash of '29. Moved to Lake Washegama after the banks took everything but the weekend house and the jewelry on Dorothy's fingers.

Laura did the math in her head again. Assuming Dorothy was eighteen when she was married, she would have been born in 1892, *five years before Dracula was released, for crying out loud.* If Dorothy wasn't in some perpetual sundowning state and had at least some of the details right, that would make her 122 years old—or just about the oldest person ever recorded. And the kicker was this: Dorothy Loney's story *did* add up, except that she couldn't possibly be 122. *Except what if she was?* thought Laura while the stacks of paperwork on her desk rearranged itself like the Chicago skyline on a building spree.

The Regulator over Madelene's desk tick-tocked the morning away, until that great, big windup could release the pitch at noon. When she wasn't eating at her desk or treating herself to a chain-restaurant lunch special, she sometimes ate with the residents in the common room. It made them more human, and, in seeking out the lonely ones, she found people that appreciated the company. She'd eaten with Dorothy more than once, but not for a while. That was where she heard all the stories about where she was when she'd heard president McKinley had been shot, or what it was like to see the doughboys come home after The Great War.

It was baked chicken of a sort. Mashed potatoes and steamed vegetables. *As flavorless a mass as was ever served*, thought Laura, who would have brought it up to the nutritionist, but the fact was that Madelene's menus were perfectly healthy, even for those with restricted diets—and that was most of them—and pardoning herself so often of the expression ... just what the doctor ordered. Laura thought that it might have been boiled together in a big pot, and then separated on the plate to give some semblance of an actual meal, because everything tasted the same. Easy to cut, even across the table, but bland as hell, washed down with tepid coffee and dry creamer.

"Tell me about your husband," said Laura, tucking a bite of chicken (or was it a floret of broccoli?) into her cheek. As conversation starters went, didn't earn Laura any glamor points, but getting the elderly to reminisce was like shooting fish in a barrel.

"Alf was a dear, I suppose," she said. "But all men are the same, you know? Men just take on the flavor of the things around them." She smiled her gummy smile. "Like this food. It all tastes the same."

Laura knew Dorothy was speaking in general terms, but it sounded like she was talking about Laura's ex-husband, Denny, or any of the gentlemen that she had dated since—something that was more ancient history now than recent.

"He gave me a good life, though, even after we lost everything in the crash," said Dorothy in something of a sigh. It didn't sound wistful. It was just a sigh, like she wasn't getting enough oxygen and wanted to keep herself from graying out like she did sometimes.

"How are you feeling, Missus Loney?"

"A little tired," she admitted. "But when you're my age, it happens."

"And how old are you?" asked Laura. "If you don't mind my asking?"

"I—I don't remember. What year is it?"

Dorothy was feeling a little tired, as she called it, because of her anemia. She was probably due for another blood transfusion, but she would have to double check the charts to make sure. She felt a little bad for not remembering, but ... *that's why they keep charts!*

"Are you happy here?"

"Sure, dear," said Dorothy. "My thinking is: you bring your happiness with you."

"You don't miss your husband?"

"Of course I do!" she answered, the smile-crinkles bunching. "But I have to admit—I miss the sun more. What I wouldn't give to feel it on my skin again, you know? I think I'd like that better than running in the grass—grass with dew still on it. Oh, how I remember that. My, when I was a little girl, oh, the running I would do. You wouldn't believe..."

Laura smiled, trying to remember when the last time it was that *she* ran over the grass, still heavy with dew. Treadmills, yes. Sidewalks and along curbs, you bet. But running through the grass was something kids did, and that was years and years ago. The closest she came was mowing her sister's lawn while her sister was nursing a broken foot—and that had been August, when the grass was hard and sharp and riddled with thistles. Her grandmother used to say that *time had wings like trees had rings*, and Laura wondered what she would see if she could look inside Dorothy Loney.

"Would you like me to wheel you over there?"

"Heavens, no!" said Dorothy so quickly, it belied her age-related deafness. A trembling hand reached for her coffee and curled around the mug, her fingers looked like chains, knobby, but imposing.

"Oh, okay—"

She finished a ginger sip, and her eyes slowly focused to the sharp dentition of canine teeth. "It would be the end of me, my dear."

Anything might be the end of you, thought Laura, the creep of shame reaching over her for imagining such a thing. "No, Missus Loney. You'll outlive us all. You just watch." But the words, however cheap, felt genuine, even if she didn't really mean them.

"I hope not," said Dorothy, her knuckly hands still wrapped around the mug of coffee while it sat on the table. She held onto it like she meant it, but didn't want anyone to know—like if she let go, she might slip away, which seemed counter-intuitive after what she had said about not wanting to live forever.

But then, thought Laura, *wanting to die right now was a lot different than wanting to die someday.*

"Time is like money, and if you have too much of it, it's like ... like—" Here she paused, blowing the dust off of some mislaid and long-forgotten memory. "I can't remember the word, I don't think, but it's like German money between the wars. Printed so much of it to pay off their debts, it was worthless. They were using it for notepaper. Do you want to do that to the calendar of your own life? Tear off the pages to wipe your rear end?"

Inflation is the word you're looking for, thought Laura. I learned that word when I was a little girl—when Jimmy Carter was president, and there were long lines at the gas stations. Laura remembered her parents and grandparents grousing about it, but it didn't mean anything to her in her pigtails. It was a time so far removed from now, that it had almost as much meaning as those Weimar Republic banknotes she hadn't thought about since world history in high school. All she could say in response was, 'No,' while she wagged her head like a perpetual motion machine.

"Of course you don't," said Dorothy, sipping from her coffee mug again and smacking her lips over her toothless gums. "Neither do I. Neither do I. But sometimes it feels like I'm just knitting away eternity."

Laura peered far into the future, when she might live at a place called Golden Oakes, instead of just working there. She thought she could see, sitting on the horizon in a wheelchair of her own, her future self. *Still single, I bet,* she thought, and wondered why that was so important to her. It made her wonder how long Dorothy had been single, and while she didn't think it was the best form to ask, she couldn't help herself. "How long ago did your husband die?"

"Alf died in 1963, the same year Kennedy was shot."

More than half a century, and yet, Dorothy could recall it as easily—no, *more* easily—than what she had for breakfast that morning ... if she had anything other than coffee, which she probably didn't. And that recalled the anecdote Dorothy shared with her once about the lunchpail she carried with her to school when she lived on Sheffield in Chicago.

That lunchpail fascinated Laura, and after much cross-examination over a longitudinal series of conversations, Laura had that memory firmly planted in the year 1898, the year the good old U.S. of A. went to war with Spain, and Teddy Roosevelt charged up San Juan Hill with the Roughriders.

Thankfully, Dorothy had no memory of that. Still, the memory of the lunchpail was a shocking 116 years old. Making that letter from President Bush—the first president Bush—seem that much more genuine. *Still*, she thought, *it couldn't be.*

After lunch, Laura wheeled Dorothy back to the window where she could watch the afternoon sunshine bend away from her on the floor, rolling over the low pile of the industrial carpeting. She cast a look over her shoulder, and caught a glimpse of Dorothy starting another row on the scarf she was knitting. Her hundredth. Or maybe her thousandth.

Back at her desk, Laura checked the charts—Dorothy's anemia required regular, if not often, blood transfusions, and her red blood count was dipping down again. The tables didn't lie, and she tapped the lowly number with her fingernail with the beat of a funeral drum. *What would happen if she didn't get her transfusion?* she wondered, answering in her mind so quickly and faintly that it felt like an echo in a different voice: *she would just fade away.* And without a 'Do not Resuscitate' order in place, that could get pretty sticky—from a legal standpoint, anyway.

And then Laura felt it. An itch. It wasn't anywhere on her body. It was somewhere she couldn't reach with her hands—her mind. It started as a feather tickle, and like any really good itch, it pretty much stayed that way. And stayed. And stayed. And stayed some more. She wanted to rake her nails across it like when she tore into her husband's back on her wedding night, *Freddy Krueger-style*, she added, picturing the fedora-wearing burn victim with his trademark wicked grin and claw-gloves. *What does it say about me that I'm seeing Freddy and not Wolverine?* she thought, shrugging, not just in her mind, but in fact. Jerry didn't notice. Madelene wasn't in the room. She had gotten away with it, and now it was time to run her streak to two.

She walked out of the office like she was sneaking. If Jerry (or Madelene, should she return), or anyone else even noticed, they *wouldn't* notice. Laura walked in and out of the office all the time. But because she had an off the books task to complete, she felt like she was glowing the 'Action Green' of the Seattle Seahawks uniform piping—the kind of color that only shoe executives and freshwater fish find enticing.

Dorothy was sitting near the window, knitting another row on what looked like the same scarf she was always working on but never finished.

But of course that was absurd—it would be a ridiculous Rapunzel-length by now, something worthy of Tom Baker on *Doctor Who*. Dorothy didn't seem to notice Laura as she approached, but she *felt* noticed. The hairs on her arms stood up, reverse dominoes almost invisible in the sunlight. She smoothed them down, but the goose pimples wouldn't go away. There was something she had to do, and she wasn't sure if she was right, wrong, or just plain crazy for doing it.

The wheelchair was an old one, very old, a basic model that staff kept comfortable for Dorothy by layering it with cushions and pillows, and had anyone else been sitting in it, it would probably have been used by several, maybe even dozens of people before it got to Dorothy, the Methuselah of Golden Oakes. The brakes were still locked. If dusted, they would be covered in Laura's prints. No one had touched her since lunchtime. Laura had no way of knowing this, but she just *knew*. Things were lining up.

When she pulled the brakes back, Dorothy stiffened a little, like she knew what was happening, but she didn't say anything to Laura. She just kept on knitting, maybe a little faster than before.

Sunshine is the key to this, thought Laura. *Light and truth. Both expose the darkness.* It felt like something out of a Sunday school lesson, and it felt *true*. If she said as much to Dorothy, she was sure she would agree. There was something not quite right about Dorothy, or maybe the world Laura was reaching for was 'natural'. Nobody ever lived that long, and it felt like a cosmic mistake, like God lost Dorothy's file behind the cabinet, and just now slapped his head and said 'Oh, shit, Dorothy Loney! I forgot all about her!' Laura imagined it sounded like a thunderclap.

The wheelchair creaked as the wheels turned. It seemed to Laura like they had been sleeping, and it rolled forward like it had woken up from a nap—groggy and unwilling, wishing hard to return to stasis. The resistance went all the way up Laura's arms, and she had to fight to push it forward, even though there was nothing in the way, no physical resistance at all. Laura looked around to see if anyone was watching. If anyone were, they would think nothing of it, but the guilty heat seeped up from her collar, and the sweat smelled foul.

"You ever wonder how I eat?"

Laura stopped pushing the wheelchair. The question 'what?' lodged in her throat, but her pause was enough.

"With no teeth, I mean. And no dentures."

"I just—I assumed..."

Dorothy's frail frame started to turn with the reluctance of paper mache, dry and with a hint of crackling, reminding Laura of the Egyptology exhibit at the Field Museum that had filled her childhood with so much fascination and dread. "How can I bite my food?"

Laura couldn't see her face, but she could hear the smile in her voice—

the *I know something you don't know* tone that would have been as taunting in someone four generations younger. "No, I—I actually have no idea, now that you mention it, Missus Loney." She leaned over Dorothy's inside shoulder, more to speak into her good ear, but also to see her face. It was always easier to communicate when you could see someone's face, whether they were children or supercentenarians. But it wasn't just that. Laura wanted to see. *To see.*

Dorothy was still smiling, drawing the wrinkles of her face back like a curtain. The black hole of her mouth, usually rimmed with the pale pink of barren gums, now had the crenelation of white points, like tiny shark teeth, fringing them on the top and bottom. The teeth were so small, it looked like white lace, but they were sharp, serrated. Those teeth were made for slicing. Baked chicken and broccoli didn't stand a chance.

"My God—what are they?" said Laura, grasping for a rational explanation. False teeth. Bits of food stuck to her gums. Or maybe Laura's own insanity.

"They're my *fangs*, sweetheart," said Dorothy in a whisper that was loud and clear but only Laura seemed to hear. "They're to drink blood—but I haven't had a proper meal in forever. Since Alf died in 1963, I think. Now they call me 'anemic' and pump me full of fresh blood. It's not as enjoyable as drinking it, but it keeps me going—just enough to sit and knit."

Laura shook her head, not sure if she was disagreeing with some delusion, or trying to shake the delusion from her own head. Her jaw waggled she shook it so hard, feeling like a dog trying to whip the life out of a rabbit caught in the yard. A dog with sharp teeth.

Like Dorothy's.

Dorothy's eye twinkled, and the creases stretched even further. "It's true, whether you believe it or not. But when you've been on a drip diet like I have for as long as I have, you're not afraid to prove it. Where were you taking me just now?"

Laura looked at the yellow patch of sunlight on the floor.

"Take me there. You do it, honey. Go ahead."

The wheelchair creaked noiselessly, but Laura could feel the vibrations through the handles in her hands. The chair itself was more reluctant than Dorothy, and Laura was the most reluctant of all, but she couldn't stop. It was like struggling against a free-fall.

"It'll be fine, dear," said Dorothy, dropping the scarf, now complete, in the shadow as she passed into the light. "Leave it be," she said, her loose skin going nearly invisible in the full blast of the afternoon sunshine. "Until after..."

"After what?"

"My Uncle Gerhard immigrated like the rest of us, but he went back," said Dorothy. "And forth. He was a fruit picker in California, like in those

Steinbeck stories. Worked in the railyards in Detroit. And the oil fields in Texas."

There was an electrical smell in the air, like ozone, faint but distinct that made Laura's nostrils flare involuntarily, but she was less interested in it than she was the reverie that Dorothy found herself on at the moment.

"He came back home with something," said Dorothy. "A disease. Most men, it would be a venereal disease, but not Gerhard. He had the plague. *The* plague, and it wasn't bubonic. Old Gerhard walked in one night out of the blue—I hadn't seen him for a couple of years. I thought he was tired. His skin was worn out and drawn, but when I saw his teeth. Mercy, they looked like Lon Chaney's in *London After Midnight*. Razor sharp, like those little fish in the Amazon. The ones can eat whole cows?" She bunched up her fists like she wanted to snap but the arthritis wouldn't let her, and they trembled in her lap.

"Piranhas?"

"That's it," said Dorothy.

Laura looked down at the old woman in her house dress, at the shaking fists that shook with the tremens of extreme old age. And that's when Laura saw the filaments of smoke seeping out from between Dorothy's arthritic knuckles. It looked so much like the strands of a spiderweb at first that Laura thought she had rolled her through the first tendrils of one—but there were no spiders, and the lines were vapor that smelled of electrical fire.

"Missus Loney?" she asked the old woman.

And then her fists were aflame, like a wizard in a duel, but she didn't have control of the fire—it had control of her, streaking up her arms so fast that Laura fell back dismayed. From the floor, she could only see the back of Dorothy's skull, shrunken like a nut in a haze of wispy hair that looked not unlike the smoke that had crawled from her fists before all hell broke loose. Then in another instant, it was gone, vaporized by the flames.

Overhead sprinklers rained on the room while the alarms brayed and flashed as the ambulatory residents shuffled out of the room, and the nursing staff hurried the others out in their wheelchairs. One of the orderlies sprayed Dorothy with a fire extinguisher, but she wouldn't go out, even when a second and third would-be hero doused her with blankets of foam. Dorothy wouldn't stop burning until she was *done* burning, a charcoal corpse in a melted chair still sitting by the window, enjoying the hell out of the sunshine for the first time in decades.

ROBERT DID IT
Kerry G.S. Lipp

Kerry G. S. Lipp lives in Louisville, Kentucky. He hates the sun and loves making fun of dead people. His parents started reading his stories and they've consequently booted him from their will. Kerry's work appears in several anthologies including *DOA2* from Blood Bound Books. His work has been featured multiple times on The Wicked Library podcast. He is currently editing his first novel, writing his second, and shopping a bizarro novella. Kerry rarely (but still) blogs at *Horror Tree* and will launch his own website sometime before he dies.

Say hi on Twitter @kerrylipp or come find him on Facebook. And he wants you to remember to always cover the camera on your laptop. You never know who's watching you.

They don't let you drink on the tour even though it takes place in one of the handful of American cities that allows open containers. They say it's because there are no restrooms on the tour, but I know better. They are trying to protect you. It's because when you meet *him* you might do something stupid. You might not follow the rules:
Introduce yourself
    Ask permission if you would like a photo
    Thank him afterward
    Sounds simple right? What they don't tell you is that he requires many, many other rules, but no one knows exactly what they are. His name is Robert and he is a doll, but don't let that fool you. He's a monster, a curser, a witch, a warlock, whatever you want to call him. He is evil and I know, because in February 2015, I met him face to face.
    My name is Kerry Lipp and I live in Louisville, Kentucky. I write horror, but I don't believe in the supernatural. To be honest, I don't believe in much of anything but myself, and even that is tough sometimes. But my

parents are awesome and even better than that, they are retired and spend winters in Florida.

For Christmas they bought me a plane ticket to come visit them in Key West. They wanted to take me to the Hemingway House and give me time to write. Innocent.

I started the trouble when I discovered the haunted history of the island and talked them into a midnight ghost tour that culminated in a late night rendezvous with Robert the Doll.

The tour started like I'm sure they all do. The open-air trolley picked us up and our tour guide, who called himself the Body Hooker, started telling us stories. Key West is a cool place. It's a paranormal investigator and urban legend seeker's haven.

And an alcoholic's. Don't believe me? Go read up on Hemingway.

You can't get a good mojito in Kentucky. They're all syrup and no actual mint leaves, a mistake you're allowed to make at BW3s once and never again. But it's one of my favorite drinks. You know where you can get an endless array of sizes and flavors of authentic mojito?

Key West.

My parents aren't much for the sauce, but even when it's just the three of us, I try not to let that stop me, plus, they do the driving. It works out.

We rolled into Key West in mid-afternoon with no real plans other than dinner at Blue Heaven around 7 and the ghost tour at 10. Plenty of time to take in the city and enjoy the sunset at Mallory Square.

Hemingway House and the Aquarium were scheduled for later in the week so we puttered around like clueless tourists. My parents stopped off for an ice cream cone. I declined and headed into the bamboo bar next door with a street sign boasting over 40 flavors of mojitos. I'd have been happy if I never had to leave, but vacation with your parents doesn't really include ditching them at three in the afternoon to get day wasted at a bar by yourself.

So I did what any 31-year-old semi-functioning alcoholic would do. I bought two of the strongest mojitos they sold and a normal one. I bashed the two high octane cocktails like I was back in college, caught my breath, tipped my bartender and carried my Key West original, complete with a stick of sugar cane, out to the street where I casually sipped as my folks licked their ice cream cones.

We walked and looked at the people surging across the sidewalks and arts and crafts kiosks peddling tiny palm trees and ceramic sunsets as chickens pecked their way through the streets. Yes, real chickens, they are everywhere, like pigeons in New York, but a lot more fun to watch.

My mom and pop saw a furniture store a few fronts down and are crazy enough to buy furniture in Key West for their home in Ohio. Fortunately, music boomed from an outdoor patio next door where the girls served drinks in coconut bikinis. We went our separate ways.

"You sure this is okay?" My dad asked over his shoulder.

"I think I'll make it," I said.

They disappeared into the furniture store and I abandoned my beloved mojito to take a chance on the house drink, something called a dark and stormy. It's ginger beer and dark rum. Hard to go wrong with a cocktail composed entirely of alcoholic ingredients.

It was delicious. I sipped it through a straw on the sunny patio as I watched people and chickens and when my drink ran dry I had another, and then another and I looked at my phone and realized that we had dinner reservations in fifteen minutes. We missed Mallory Square. Maybe tomorrow.

That's how it went down. I'm slugging drinks all afternoon and I still have to be the one to pull them out of the furniture store to make our dinner reservation.

What would they do without me?

We trotted through the streets jugglers and musicians until we hit the world famous Blue Heaven. With distinguished décor, fantastic food and potent potables, the fame is well earned.

We ate outside among the chickens doing their little head bob walk underneath the tables and brushing against your legs, but if you tried to pat them, they'd peck your fingers.

With full stomachs and satisfied smiles we trekked back to the car to grab jackets and sweatshirts, even in Florida February can get a little chilly at night time. Once there we bundled up and with about an hour to kill, headed to a bar called Sloppy Joe's that once served as Hemingway's second home.

A couple drinks there and I was teetering on the fine line between buzzed up and full on shitfaced, but I did my best to walk it like a tightrope as we headed to the pick-up spot where the Body Hooker and his cohorts would take us to meet Robert the Doll, the cursed creep who inspired the bloodthirsty red-headed toddler known as Chucky from the *Child's Play* franchise.

With a little anxiety and a lot more booze rumbling in my stomach I took a bench seat behind my parents in the packed house, open-air trolley while the Body Hooker introduced himself and laid out the rules of the tour. Basically three: no booze, no bathrooms, and if anyone out on the street yelled "you're doomed" at the bus, in unison, the entire bus had to respond, "yes, we are the doomed."

I thought he was nuts until drunk assholes on the streets started yelling "you're doomed," before the fucking bus even took off. In response, I did what any drunk punk on vacation with his parents would do. I led the entire bus by standing up and screaming at the top of my lungs, "yes, we are the doomed."

That scored a quizzical look from both my mom and dad, and also inspired the Body Hooker to add another rule: no standing up on the bus.

As we drove through close and crowded streets, the Body Hooker told us different legends and lore of the island. It's got a rich, haunted history as it's faced its fair share of disease, tragedy, racism, psychopathy, and curses.

Most notably, the curse of Robert the Doll.

I'll be honest, even though he's world famous, I'd never heard of him until about a month before my trip, but once I discovered him, I started seeing him everywhere. Not quite sure what that means, nor do I wish to think about it.

As I've mentioned I was pretty drunk at this point, so I don't even remember the whole story the Body Hooker told us, and I'm not here to regurgitate Robert's Wikipedia page, but I'll summarize it as best as I remember it.

Some important family on the island had a housekeeper that was Cuban or Haitian or something. The housekeeper gave the doll to that family's little boy, Robert. Little Robert was so enamored with the doll that he named him after himself. Yeah, where were the parents on that one?

Supposedly, the maid enchanted it herself with a curse or voodoo or something, and soon after gifting the doll, weird shit started to happen. Things started breaking all over the house. When confronted by his parents, Robert's response was always to point at his doll and say, "Robert did it." This became his mantra every time a vase broke or toys got destroyed.

At first the parents didn't know what to say, but later, they reported hearing giggling throughout the house, which they themselves attributed to Robert the Doll. In addition to that, many people claim to have observed the doll's facial expressions changing right in front of their eyes. Truth or bullshit, the parents finally had enough and condemned Robert the Doll to the attic.

I'll be the first to admit, at least to me, that's not all that creepy, but once you get a good look at Robert, either in person or simply a photo, just looking at the doll, even without knowing his history will shoot a chill up your spine.

And now, I was about to meet him face to face.

Cool.

The bus stopped at an old Civil War fort that looked more like a castle that serves as a museum in 2015. On the way to meet Robert the Doll, the Body Hooker told us that lots of people had been imprisoned and died here and handed us a ghost meter to see if we could detect any pulses of souls still roaming the makeshift cemetery trapped in limbo. My ghost meter didn't read anything, but it was dark and quiet and thinking about the thousands that died horrible deaths there hung heavy in the air.

They walked us around a few dirt paths and then finally to a door that led to Mr. Robert the Doll. Before turning us loose on his turf, the Body Hooker made sure that we knew the rules. Remember them? Just like the tour guide, I'm only saying them once.

Seeing the excitement lighting up my face, my mom grinned at me and jabbed me in the ribs with her elbow. In true dad fashion, my dad said, "Finally, Kerry, the maaaaaaiiiiiiin event," dragging out the word in a parody of any ring announcer.

We walked down a short hallway and there he was.

Robert the Doll resides in the middle of a room the size of a school classroom. He sits on a pedestal about four feet off the ground encased in thick glass. Not sure if it's bulletproof, but I'm positive there's an alarm. Dim light emanated from the four corners of the room, enough so that you could see things, but dark enough to cast creepy shadows in all directions.

And eerie.

And awkward.

Most of the anxious people on the tour directed their attention to the walls of the room, which are actually chalkboards where people can write messages. Not me, I wasn't interested in that. I went right up to Robert, put my face against the glass, and introduced myself.

"Hey Robert," I said. "My name is Kerry."

"Hello Robert," my dad said in a dramatic, serious dad voice.

"Hi Robert," my mom chimed in. Then, "Ask him."

I swallowed and with a boozy, lopsided grin, I asked, "Can I get a picture, Robert?"

His stoic face didn't move, at least not to my eyes, but the overall creepiness of it, his tiny, pitch-black eyes and the marks pocking his timeworn face like chickenpox scars will forever remain seared into my mind.

"May I take your picture?" My mom asked.

"Good thinking," I said, "I'd hate to get us cursed on a technicality."

My dad wandered off to read the chalkboards on the walls or people watch as I took my place in front of Robert's glass house. I smiled, big and happy as my mom held up my iPhone and took a few pictures rapid fire. She narrowed her eyes, as she studied the results, clearly not satisfied.

"I'm going to try it with the flash," she said.

She snapped another photo and I saw stars.

"That's a little better," she said, "but now there's a glare."

"It doesn't have to win a Pulitzer," I said, "I just want to look cool on Facebook."

"Don't be a smart ass," she said.

Point mom.

"Walk around back," she said. "The glass is clear, maybe it'll look better that way."

I swayed my way around Robert.

She held up the phone and snapped a couple pictures.

"Much better," she said.

I stayed there for a minute, observing Robert from behind. His white sailor hat was just about head high to me. Unable to see his face, he wasn't so scary. The little devil in my head had been drinking all day too, and he gave me an idea I couldn't ignore.

"Take one more," I said.

When she raised the phone and waited for it to focus, I shot two fingers up in a V behind Robert's head.

I gave Robert the Doll bunny ears.

She snapped the photo.

My mom made a sound somewhere between a laugh and a gasp before shaking her head and handing my phone back to me.

"That probably wasn't a great move," she said.

And as soon as the words left her, my phone slid from my hand and cracked on the ground. It didn't break, but it sounded like a gunshot in the quiet room.

"Robert did it," she smirked. "Hurry up, I want my picture too."

"Seriously?"

"Why not?"

"Okay."

She walked over and got into position. Through my drunken haze, I understood her difficulty getting a good picture. Everything about Robert and the lighting and the glass, just made things...weird, but I fired off a few pictures and finally got a passable one. She came back and together we scrolled through the pictures we'd taken. With our heads that close together, I did my best to conceal the booze on my breath.

My dad snuck up behind us, squeezed a hand on both of our shoulders and yelled, "Hey! I think it's time to get back on the bus."

We both about jumped out of our skin.

"Dammit," I muttered, but I was laughing.

"We better thank him," my mom said, "I'd be extra sincere if I were you, after that stunt you pulled."

"Hey, those bunny ears are gonna be worth at least five extra likes on Facebook."

"You gave Robert the Doll bunny ears? I thought we raised you better than that," My dad sighed and shook his head.

I shrugged, smirked, and flicked my eyes between them.

"I hope he doesn't curse ya!" My mom laughed.

"I don't believe in that hocus pocus," I said, "But I'm gonna thank him anyways."

"You better," my mom said.

The three of us thanked him and got back on the bus where the Body Hooker told us one more story about a corrupt sheriff leaving a holding cell door unlocked so the KKK could get easy access to an innocent prisoner. I only heard half the story since I was already busy uploading my photo and waiting for the cascade of likes and comments it would provoke.

After the bus dropped us off back at the beginning we decided to call it a night and head to the bed and breakfast we called home for that week. My body was tired from walking all day and my head was swimmy from too many cocktails. Even though it had been a while since my last drink, I wasn't really sobering up, it was more like a preemptive hangover setting in. I nodded off in the backseat.

I woke up to a vibrating pocket as we pulled into the parking lot. It was a Facebook message from my friend Jaime.

"Dude," it said, "Did you really give Robert the Doll bunny ears? What are you? Fucking psychotic? You're gonna pay for that one." All punctuated with an emoji winking and sticking his tongue out.

Even though I'd only been out for twenty minutes, the day of exertion drowned in booze left me fuzzy-headed and not knowing what she was talking about. Then I remembered and opened the Facebook app on my phone and saw two things. One that made me smile and another that chilled my bones. In just under an hour, my picture had generated 46 likes. I guess it pays to run with a horror driven hive-mind sometimes. What chilled me, was that in the photo, I was just standing behind Robert with a serious look on my face. No bunny ears to be seen. My arms rested at my sides, my hands not even visible.

"What the hell?" I muttered as I walked up the stairs of the bed and breakfast. I'd seen the picture, hell, I'd posted it, and so had Jaime apparently, but each time I refreshed the page, it was the same picture, no bunny ears. I wanted to answer her, but I didn't really know what to say.

I needed to pee, so I went and afterward splashed some cold water on my face. I stepped out and my parents told me goodnight and not to stay up too late, we were going fishing tomorrow morning.

"Got it," I said.

They went to their bedroom and I went to the refrigerator. One beer, I told myself. One beer and then bed. I stepped out of the kitchen and through the sliding glass door and onto the balcony where I heard faint water sloshing.

I sipped my beer and checked Facebook again. 54 likes, but still no bunny ears. I hadn't answered Jaime yet and she sent me another message. This one sent another bolt up and down my spine. "Dude, did you change the picture? There's no bunny ears now... What the hell is going on?"

I leaned my back against the sliding door and wrote back, "I have no idea. I really did give him bunny ears. My mom took the picture. That's the one I posted to Facebook, but it's different now, and I swear I didn't change it."

"Okay, that's pretty freaky," she answered.

"No shit," I wrote.

"Well you and freakiness pretty much go hand in hand. How's the rest of the trip going? I'm guessing you're not pulling mad island girl ass with your parents across the hall..."

I laughed out loud, but closed the chat window. I had an idea. The bunny ears picture was gone from Facebook, but it still had to be in my photos. All I had to do was find it, and I could prove to myself that I wasn't drunk or crazy or cursed.

But it wasn't there.

There were about ten photos my mom had snapped off of Robert and me and not a single one of them resembled the bunny ears photo I'd uploaded to Facebook only hours ago. Nerves kicked in and my stomach started wringing itself like a twisted towel. How was this possible?

Jaime sent more messages, but I ignored them.

Instead, I scrolled through the photos again, found the same one that was on Facebook, the same one that had the bunny ears two hours ago and I studied it and studied it. Then a new idea hit me, I could zoom in, maybe I just couldn't see the ears because my eyes weren't working from this distance, so I put my thumb and index finger in the screen and pulled them apart. The photo zoomed way in, right on Robert's face and then I saw them, clear as vodka, my two fingers poking out from behind his head, but right in front of my eyes they faded, then disappeared.

"What the..." I said aloud.

And then from the picture on my phone, Robert the Doll winked at me.

I screamed as the beer bottle fell from my fingers and shattered on the concrete patio overlooking the Gulf of Mexico.

My parents came rushing out, throwing open the glass sliding door. They took one look at me, and another at the shattered glass.

"What the hell is going on out here?" My dad asked.

"I uh..." I looked at my phone, then at the ground, then up at them.

"Let me guess," my mom said, "Robert did it."

I opened my mouth, then closed it, smiled, and went inside to find a broom.

JUST LIKE EVERYTHING ELSE
Stephen Millard

Stephen Millard is a writer of prose, poetry, and music. He hails from the heartland of Kansas and now lives in the San Bernardino mountains of Southern California where he awaits the return of his fiancé, a marine; his work is a reflection of her. His first collection of poetry will be available near the first of the year.

For more, go to Facebook.com/stephenmillardofficial.

My wife is dying.

Has been for a while now but I can't stop reminding myself. I tell it like a prayer as I go to bed and like an alarm as I wake up.

I tell it to myself at 8am when I give her the first pills of the day with breakfast, then again at noon for lunch and more pills, and again with dinner. I tell it to myself when I load her into the wheel chair and push it outside our home in the sun, which has seemed to hide himself as of late. I hear it in her words, those low mumbling, drooling sounds that gurgle up from the death already inside of her. But I hear it loudest when, just before bed, I bathe her, lifting her frail lifeless limbs one by one into the steaming water. Her skin, once so beautiful and vibrant is now so tarnished and thin, none of it seeming to be attached anymore. As if it's a size too big it hangs from her, twisting in my grasp, making her hard to hold on to. This act once would've been so erotic, a sexual indulgence, but now I hate it and tears fall, rippling the water, and I bathe her in them. She doesn't seem to notice, though one time a while back she met my watering eyes, and sang to them.

It was her idea initially that we open a Bed & Breakfast out and away from everything. Many just thought that we couldn't come by an actually decent location and our families always asked, 'Why there?' but she wanted it. She wanted it and I said 'Yes love, of course we can.' So here we made our home and our livelihood.

It was good for a while, really was and everyone was shocked. Then, just like everything else it changed, and with a new highway went the travelers and we've been the only ones to sleep here for quite a while. Sure some folks come by every now and again but if we weren't already retired with this place paid off we would've had to leave as well.

It used to be so lovely, I handled the business side of it and she handled everything else. Cooked, cleaned, hell she hand stitched every curtain in this place. We had a damn good time but now... I'm nearly eighty-years-old and for the first time in my life I vacuum and cook and wash dishes and of course, there's no longer any business to tend to. It's all backwards now. Backwards because my wife is dying.

I feel more tears forming themselves, dangling their truth in front of me as I kneel at her bedside. She's sleeping, gently. She always slept gently these days. I reach out and grab her hand and as the first of who knows how many tears falls down onto the floor I hear the knocker rapping at the front door. I turn an ear towards it, flicking a tear off with the motion, then look up at the clock. 2:45 pm.

As I get up, listening to myself creak, I wonder how long it's been since anyone came around, but it's been too long to remember. Descending the steps to the main floor I think I should just take the sign from the roadside and turn off the light above the door. But with her handwriting on that sign I know I never will.

I get to the door and hear her groan from upstairs.

With pinched lips to stop their quivering I open the door, relieved to find that no one is there. I look left and right, then out at the dirt road leading up to the house and see no car. Again relief fills me, I can go back to her now. Back to the last decrepit evidence that I had happiness once.

I close the door and turn around to find a man standing before me. I don't jump or scream or react much at all, I just look at him, confused.

"Hello, Tom," he says. I am taken back, only our last names adorn the sign.

"How do you do?" I reply. He nods, taking off a ten gallon hat and as he sits, he caps it on one knee. It rests just above where his leather boot stops. "I didn't see you come in I thought you were..." I smile, slightly embarrassed, pointing with a thumb back at the door.

"I let myself in, sorry if I startled you, I know you don't get many guests anymore," his eyes stay in mine, "but my how you've kept up with the place." His face is nearly emotionless aside from one. Is it pity? Or is he just overcome with his apology? I doubt the latter.

"I didn't see your car outside, are you hitching?" This used to be very common. He just shakes his head, a man of few words. I stand there as he examines my eyes.

"...Well then," I say growing uncomfortable, "we have three rooms-"

"I won't be needing a room," he says. His voice is gentle, but there is something terrible about him I can't place. My look of confusion begs him to explain.

"I'm here for something else," my brow furrows as this is no explanation at all.

"Listen mister I don't know who you are but-"

"Yes you do," with a delicate interruption he barely manages a smile. It looks unnatural on him, as if he's trying it for the first time.

"There's no money here," my voice stern now, I'm growing sick of his intimidating bullshit.

"You really don't know me?" He's hurt, like a child whose mother has forgotten him. His lack of maturation is paralleled by his weathered country appearance. Along with his boots and hat he wears a shiny round belt buckle that keeps a flannel shirt tucked into faded blue jeans.

"'Fraid not," I reply. He just looks at me, surprised that I'm missing something. "Just state your business sir. At my age I have no time for games." She groans again from upstairs, his eyes become suddenly alert.

"Is that Rose?"

"She is no business of yours. Now will you please-"

"Can I see her?"

"No you may not." I stand as upright as my tired old spine will let me. He stands up, not intimidated. "You'll sit back down if you know what's good for you." He turns and begins walking toward the staircase. The sound of a shotgun cocking stops him. He looks back towards me, his face so blank. Two hands put his hat back on after which he tilts his head like a curious dog.

"Yeah that got your attention," I can't help but grin like I'm Clint Eastwood. "Now you just walk on out of here son."

"But, I haven't gotten what I need yet."

"And that's a shame." We just look at each other.

"I'm going upstairs." His voice is laced with a child's vindication.

"And I'm going to put a hole in your back. There's nothing up there for you."

"Yes, there is," he turns and begins up the stairs. The gun goes off before I realize, spraying destruction his way. He turns around to face me, unchanged.

"Do you know who I am now?" I look around him, seeing the hole I just put in the staircase behind him. "The boss says I should start wearing black. Says it might be easier for people to understand." The barrel fades down to the ground, I feel my heart pump grief to my eyes.

"No," I whimper, "No, no, no."

"I'm sorry," he genuinely is.

"You can't be." I can barely hear my voice.

"I am. But I promise it won't hurt." He turns around. I cock again and empty another shell his way, only to put another hole in the stairs and this time, failing to delay him a bit. He gets halfway up the stairs before I throw the gun down to pursue him. I can't let her be alone for this.

Even at his leisurely pace he is quicker getting up than I and the sobs come. I avoid the holes and hold the railing, dropping tiny splashes of pleading sadness along the way. He's standing at her side when I get to them.

"Please," I can't stand it, "one more day, just give her one more day." I fall to my knees, pain shoots up but I don't care. My hands clasp together.

His soft apologetic eyes move to me.

"Goddammit please!" He looks back at her, taking off his hat and holding it with two hands against his chest. Thoughts appear of me cleaning and cooking for only myself, flashes of a miserable existence without my wife of 58 years.

He moves one hand towards her. I scream out as death touches her forehead, a reaction to watching her die. But he just brushes hair off her clammy forehead, her chest continuing to rise and fall.

"I thought..."

"People have the worse conceptions of us."

"Us?" These conceptions I clearly share.

"You thought I'd be the only one." I stare at him staring at her. "No, someone else will be along shortly for her." He discontinued his touch and put his hat back on, again with two hands.

"Someone else," I now understand jubilantly, "so you're here just to what...survey her?" He looks at me with more pity than ever.

"I'm not here for her." A new weight hits me, taking all the solace I had mistaken like a mirage. I look from the man to my wife and back. "But like I said she'll be fine without you until-"

"What?" I can't understand. He pulls out a watch from his pocket and flips it open, then looks back at me without a word. "Please just leave," I say crying again.

"We will, and she'll follow soon after. In her sleep," he looks back at her, "that's how most say they'd like to go." I stand up, weakly moving to the bed. "We're out of time," he says.

I crawl onto it, pulling her into my arms with a tragically peaceful realization. I close my eyes with tears and a smile.

"I thought I'd die without her."

COLLECTED POEMS
K.A. Opperman

K.A. Opperman's work has appeared in *Spectral Realms* (*Hippocampus Press*), *Necronomicum*, various anthologies from *Horrified Press*, and will appear in *Weird Fiction Review*, *Nameless Digest*, and *Xnoybis*. His debut verse collection, *The Crimson Tome* (*Hippocampus Press*) is currently available.

The Shadow of the Reaper

I saw the Reaper in his purple robe
Reflected in my wineglass yesternight:
His grinning death's-head gleamed a ghastly white,
His bony hand reached forth my soul to probe.

I turned to face that grim dark angel, Death—
But there was naught behind me but the drapes
Of dull red velvet, forming dreadful shapes
As they did stir in nightwind's cold, black breath....

I tried to hide among the gala guests
That danced beneath the crystal chandelier—
And yet between two lovers drawing near,
Again I glimpsed the Reaper, Lord of Pests.

He fixed me with his icy, eyeless gaze,
And held aloft in one decrepit hand
A wingèd hourglass, whose emblackened sand
Had nearly drained the dregs of all my days!

Now all the gladsome guests have gone, and I—
I am alone. The darkness closes in,
And in the gloom I see a graveyard grin

With rotted teeth, and roaches in each eye.

The booming chimes of midnight sound my doom—
The shadow of his scythe is on the wall,
And like the clock-hand's slow yet certain fall—
It lowers over harvest for the tomb!

The Lady of the Graves

Who mourns the long departed,
Whom no salvation saves?
It is the mournful-hearted
Dark Lady of the Graves.

Whose kiss makes red each marker
On ways the tombstone paves?
No dress than hers is darker—
The Lady of the Graves.

Her wan and lace-veiled weeping
The ivied granite laves.
Red roses there are heaping—
Sweet Lady of the Graves!

Her black-beglovèd fingers
Caress what death engraves
On stone that coldly lingers,
Dear Lady of the Graves.

I almost think I love her,
Who ghouls and gargoyles braves,
With Dian's horns above her!—
Good Lady of the Graves!

I pray that when I perish,
Where silver willow waves,
My memory she'll cherish—
My Lady of the Graves.

A WITCH'S TALE
Jennifer A. Smith

Jennifer A. Smith writes tales of horror and unease. She was born in Minnesota during the second half of the twentieth century. A childhood love of reading, along with a penchant for old horror films, has awakened a love for the dark and unholy; thirty years of working at a small town post office have nourished that obsession.

I'm not really a witch, although I apparently have all of the trappings of one. I live in a cottage in the forest, I'm an older woman with grey hair and I'm a bit of a recluse. I manage pretty well through most of the year but when the autumn rolls around, well, all bets are off. Suddenly my reputation as a woman of evil repute resurfaces and the early sunsets and the excitement regarding Halloween builds to an unhealthy level. And during October, I find children skirting my cottage, looking fearfully at me while I gather herbs and flowers.

My grandmother lived in this cottage years ago and she left it to me upon her death. I had a great affinity for her and her way of life and we got along famously. My mother said that it skipped a generation because she was a city girl. She left the country cottage as soon as she possibly could. She had a scholarship to a college in New York City and she loved it there. She met my father in college and they lived a life of big city proportions. They both did quite well in their chosen fields and owned a nice apartment in Manhattan. But that was no life for me. I relished the summers spent with my granny in her cottage in the woods. She taught me the names of the birds, the insects, and all of the amazing plant life. She had a book of medicinal herbs that she kept, planning on publishing it someday when natural medicine came back into vogue. She was a great believer in the changing of the fads in everyday life. "Look at the rising of interest in midwives and doulas, the real will come back in style again" she said often.

Well, I suffered through the years of life in the big city. I took trains and subways and ate at bustling restaurants and listened to my parents friends talk about the glories of living in NYC and how they could never leave it. I kept my own counsel and didn't betray in the slightest how differently I felt about it.

But the days after I graduated from my exclusive high school were spent in putting off my parents while they pushed me to apply to a university. I had planned for years to move with my grandmother in New England but I was afraid of their reaction and I put off giving them the news for almost a month. And I waited too long because before that month was over, we received news that Grandma had passed away. The attorney called our home and after speaking with my mother, she handed the phone to me saying "he wants to speak with you, Alison". She looked quizzically at me as I took the telephone from her.

"Miss Alison, I am your grandmother's attorney, Andrew Lewis. I wanted to express my sympathy for your loss and to tell you that your grandmother spoke of you so often that I almost feel as if I know you. She has left you all her worldly possessions, including the cottage and the acreage. There is also enough money for you to live on for many years if you live frugally, as she assured me was your wont", he said kindly. "I took the liberty of informing your mother and she seemed a little confused about it. Perhaps she didn't know of your close relationship with your grandmother."

I felt the tears welling up into my eyes as I saw my vision of the future crumbling before me. Grandma and I had always spoken of the day that I would live with her in the tiny cottage but now that had been taken from me. I thanked him and asked him what he needed from me.

The attorney said "Well, Alison, she has already been cremated and her ashes await you. She wished for you to scatter them in her garden. Then I would need for you to decide whether you wish to keep the property or sell it. I would like for you to come here and look at the place and sign a few papers. Then, of course a decision would need to be made. I understand that you are 18, so the final decision rests with you."

I thanked him and slowly hung up the phone. My parents were looking at me strangely, apparently waiting for me to explain this odd development. I also noticed that my mother had no tears in her eyes. She had evidently cut most of her ties with grandma years ago.

"Well, grandma left her cottage to me and some money. I'm going to take the train to Massachusetts and move into the cottage. I've been trying to tell you for a month that I planned to do that. Only I thought she would be with me. But I plan to live there even though she is gone," I said as forcefully as possible.

"What are you talking about? You want to go live in a ramshackle hut in the woods in the middle of nowhere. Do you think we sent you to the best schools in NYC for you to give up on the modern world and live as an high school graduate in the middle of nowhere?" she said angrily. My father didn't say anything but he showed his solidarity with my mom's opinion by nodding furiously and holding her hand.

"I'm sorry, but if you guys would have paid any attention to who I really was, this wouldn't be such a surprise to you. I've spent every summer with grandma my whole life. I love the way she lived, I couldn't stand to go on living if I was like you two!" I responded angrily.

"Well that's ridiculous", my father snapped. "You are going to attend a good college, right here in the city. How do you think you will pay for the train to Massachusetts? I certainly won't give you a cent to help you throw your whole life away!"

"I have money Dad, grandma had an account for me because she feared that something like this would happen and that you would react in this very way. I am going to the cottage, and I am going to live there. It's been my dream for as long as I can remember," I replied.

There was a lot more back and forth arguing but in the end, what could they do? But it was with very ill grace that they said their goodbyes. "You'll be back," my mother said. "I lived there and it's not what you think it is. It's a hard life and your grandmother was gossiped about for as long as I can remember. The townspeople think she's a witch. How do you think they will treat you?"

I carried my suitcase down to the waiting taxi. I didn't bring that much because I didn't think I would need all that much for my new life. I brought a few favorite books and some jeans and tee shirts. I could always send for more later if I needed it.

The taxi let me off in front of Grand Central Station. I purchased my train ticket and only had to wait for about half an hour before my train was ready for boarding. I hurried into the train looking for an empty compartment I found one with only one other person in it and I sat down happily, took my book from my purse and settled into a pleasant train ride.

I arrived much sooner than I had imagined. I suppose that the trips I taken when I was a child seemed much longer because I was so excited to see my gran. I was excited just the same but I was also a little nervous about what sort of hoops I'd have to jump through before the house was mine. I also feared that the attorney would try to talk me out of keeping the property like my parents had.

That turned out not to be the case at all. Mr. Lewis was waiting for me at the station and he greeted me most pleasantly. He said, "I knew you wouldn't want to waste any time at my office, so I have all of the paperwork with me and we can go directly to your property."

As we turned into the lane that led to Grandma's cottage, I felt awash with emotions both sad and happy. It was the most beautiful place on earth and it was kept up beautifully; It certainly wasn't a shack like my parents had said. I said , "Mr. Lewis, Grandma must not have been ill for very long, it looks as good as it ever did. Was she taking care of it herself?"

The attorney replied "As a matter of fact, she was taking care of it all herself. She actually died in her garden while she was doing some weeding. The doctors said she wouldn't have felt a thing. Her heart just stopped and she fell into her flower bed. The only reason she was found so quickly was that the milkman had been doing his rounds and she didn't come to the door when he knocked. He looked for her in her garden and found her there. As far as I know she didn't have any weakness or illness at all before the final moments."

The moment I walked into the cottage again, I knew that I was home. This was the life I had craved and dreamt of for years. And though my gran was gone, I could still feel her presence everywhere. I wouldn't call it haunting but she was there and she whispered in my ear when I needed her advice.

I took over her bedroom at the top of the stairs. I didn't change a thing. I loved the patchwork quilt and the lacy curtains. Her library took up most of the house. Every wall was covered with bookshelves and filled with every type of book imaginable. I made the guest room, my former room, into my knitting room and the kitchen was where grandma and I had made our tonics and salves.

I lived in the cottage for the next 20 years, happily and almost uneventfully. Except, as I said earlier, except in the autumn, when the leaves were blowing and the nights were getting cooler and Halloween approached. Then there was a sudden flurry of interest in me. I suppose I was the closest thing that the children had to a scary old witch. And it made me nervous, even though the time of witch burnings and hangings had long since passed, I still got a chill when I saw people cross to the other side of the street when I was in town. Maybe if I died my hair, I had gone grey prematurely and I didn't see the point of dying my hair. I probably could have come up with a natural solution by looking through grandma's book but I wasn't trying to impress anyone and my appearance was my own concern, wasn't it?

As September hurried into October, I enjoyed burning wood in the fireplace again. I had plenty of wood that I had gathered from my own wooded acreage. I started canning my vegetables and drying my herbs, preparing for the onslaught of snow and cold winds. I avoided town as much as possible during October, just on general principle and not a small amount of dread. But I still needed to go to the grocery store to lay in some supplies that I couldn't grow for myself. I needed paper products and chicken and hamburger for the freezer. I even liked to stop into the record shop to pick up music for my cd player.

I climbed on my bicycle and rode the two miles to the town. I heard the children humming the wicked witch song from *The Wizard of Oz* as I passed them on the street. I never confronted them, I just avoided them but maybe that was the wrong way to handle it. I entered the small grocers, hearing the bell above the door ring as I passed inside. Everyone in the store looked up and I swear some of them shivered. I filled my basket with the products that I needed and ignoring the pointed glances at me, walked up to the cash register. The proprietor, Joe Simpson, looked anywhere but in my eyes and gave me a total that I owed him. I paid him and pocketed the change. As I turned from the counter and headed to the door, I could feel the eyes of everyone in the store looking at me. I resisted the urge to look down and meekly slink towards the door; instead I straightened my posture and looked at the people that were staring at me and most of them had the decency to look away.

I carried my grocery tote out to my bike and loaded everything in the basket. I still felt a little shaky from the uncomfortable moment in the store and I prayed that I wouldn't fall over as I got onto my bike and rode away, back to my sweet cottage and away from the unfriendly villagers.

I rode away swiftly, if not elegantly, putting as much space between me and the village of Rushton as I possibly could. I took my groceries into my cozy house and put them neatly away. Trying to put my experience in the village out of my mind, I turned on the radio in the kitchen and took some soup from the fridge and started to heat it up on the stove. The local news was on and the newsman's voice sounded a bit stressed as he told of the disappearance of a local boy. He had gone off on his bicycle last night and had not returned home. I felt the blood rush to my face as I realized the possible implications of this. Was that why people had looked at me so strangely? Did they suspect that the "witch of Rushford" had stolen a child? "Surely not" I murmured to myself. They couldn't think that I would kidnap a child.

It wasn't even Halloween yet, it wouldn't be for several weeks. But the autumn was in full force and the sun was setting, the winds beginning to howl. I shivered and told myself not to be ridiculous. All they could do was call the police if they had suspicions, they wouldn't come with torches and tar and feathers. After all I'd lived here for almost 20 years and nothing like this had happened before. I didn't even know the child, Nathan something or other, that had been reported missing. Surely I had no reason to be afraid.

But fearful I was, that feeling of waiting for the other shoe to drop. If I only had some friends in the village. If only I could telephone someone and get reassurances that no one was suspecting me of any terrible crime. But I'd never felt the need for friends before; I'd never thought I would need any of them and so I hadn't even tried to connect with any of them. I guess I knew Agnes at the Library more than anyone else. It felt too strange to think of actually picking up my telephone and making contact, it sounded like I would be asking for trouble.

So I did nothing but light a fire in the fireplace and lie down with my current book. I sipped my soup from a large earthenware mug and tried to forget my misgivings and probably baseless fears. And slowly I did relax, eventually falling into a doze on the soft couch.

I awoke suddenly to strange sounds. There was the sound of a loud rapping on my door. I felt really confused and suddenly afraid. I quickly fell to the floor, hiding in front of the couch, pretending that I wasn't there. What a frightening feeling, knowing that someone was outside of my cottage, hammering on the door. Had they come with torches like in an old horror film? Was I about to be lynched for my suspected involvement of child abduction? I imagined the depictions of witches being burnt at the stake in nearby Salem and I grew even more terrified. I was totally innocent of any crime and I was going to be tormented and murdered because of my unusual lifestyle. How horribly ironic. I stayed where I was and continued to hide as I heard them screaming my name. And I suddenly felt the heat and heard the crackling of fire above me in the upstairs. But I didn't dare get up from my hiding place. I started to have trouble breathing and just before I lost consciousness I heard my grandma's voice. "Allison, please don't be afraid. The villagers are not here to hurt you. They are trying to help you. Our cottage has caught fire from a lightning strike." I smiled up at her and felt her love and concern flow through me. I suddenly realized that I was looking down at my body. I could see myself lying on the floor near the couch. I smiled at my grandmother who had taken my hand and she gently urged me up, up into the beautiful sky.

THE PROCESSION
Sean Wofford

Sean Wofford is a writer and musician from New Jersey. The stories of H.P. Lovecraft and Edgar Allen Poe sparked his interest in short fiction and horror. He is also influenced by Asian horror directors such as, Hideo Nakata, Takashi Shimizu, and Koji Shiraishi. He is currently studying at Fairleigh Dickinson University majoring in English literature and minoring in psychology. He works as a teacher's assistant and has been published in *Yellow Chair Review*, *Atrocity Exhibition*, and short-listed for the 2014 Benjamin Franklin House literary prize.

The cries and moans of killing could still be heard through the thick castle walls. Sealed and abandoned more than a century ago, many of us had forgotten about this ancient keep perched atop a hill and nestled amongst a thick copse. For others it held a strange place in their hearts and led their minds wondering through fantastic myth and lore. I stumbled upon one of its secret entrances after that Parader had knocked me into the sewers. Our town's grotesque tradition of the Procession has taken place every decade for as long as even the oldest residents can remember, but it has never gone on like this before. It's been three nights now and they are still roaming. Soaking the streets with blood.

I had been held up at my parents' house the night it started. Never ones to participate, we boarded up the windows and took refuge in our cramped basement, praying for the sound of church bells which always signaled the end. Elderly, and already quite ill from the long and hellish Italian summer, my parents passed in their sleep during the second night, almost as if they were one being. Perhaps it was from shock--from the Procession, or maybe it was some divine deliverance. My tired mind finds comfort in the latter. They died huddled together against the cellar wall, clutching each other in their dead hands. Alone inside that stuffy cellar the stench of their withering bodies engulfed my senses. I could taste it! See it! Their pale, lifeless faces catching the light from our single lamp, partially illuminating their ghastly figures like some Baroque painting. It was unbearable. On the third night, as I thought I heard the sounds from outside begin to wane, I decided to make a break for my sister's on the outskirts of the city. The August sun hung low and huge behind the gabled row homes lining the street. I had only journeyed a short distance when the Parader, an older looking fellow with the gleam of murder in his eyes, leapt at me from behind a pile of trash and corpses. I stumbled with shock and fell backward over a low railing into the open sewer, which snakes through our city like a sickly river. Even the old man was sane enough not to follow me into that fetid miasma. He leaned over the railing shouting incoherent curses as I surrendered myself to the current. I struggled to keep my head above the virulent water as it carried me farther and farther away from the center of the city. Eventually, the sewer drained out into an underground basin littered with bodies. Here, the sewage only came to my knees. I made my way to a stone ledge and followed it through the darkness for what felt like hours. The only sounds were the rush of the waterfall that brought me here and the squeaks of rats echoing off the damp and ancient looking walls. As the walkway came to a bend I felt a rush of cool air and was brought before an open door, which led to a wine cellar.

I knew immediately that I had somehow found my way inside the Castle. Not a soul has been known to have ever crossed its threshold. Tales and legends run numerous throughout the city. In the markets and schoolyards many have spoken of the Castle's myriad secrets and always with a certain air of authority and scholarship, but only to make their claims a bit more exciting. Most of us would revel in these stories, but deep down we all understood that we were wholly ignorant of the Castle's secrets. Though a few, claiming to have been touched by the divine or to have heard mystical whisperings in their ears late at night, would hold to their stories of the Castle with all the fervor of maniacs. One of my most vivid childhood memories is of such a being. Walking home late from school one dark, winter evening, a woman in rags revealed herself from within a shadowy crevice between buildings. She raised her arms to the sky and shouted, "Glory be to he who seeks eternal life by the Procession! Who cleanses the sins of man by the fire of the eternal. Glory be to the one who enters the Castle! Through the zenith of Heaven to Great One's chamber, which sits above this world and everything! Glory be! Glory be!" As I ran through the lightly falling snow I could still hear her shouting for several blocks. I've had many nightmares of this woman. The scene plays out exactly the same way, only I can't run. The woman slowly approaches my paralyzed body as she screams, "Glory! Glory be! Glory! Glory! Glory!" And just as she reaches out to grab me I wake up, every time.

This woman was strong in my thoughts as I made my way through the wine cellar and up the narrow stairs to the kitchen. I still reeked of the sewers but I had gradually grown accustomed to the scent and was able to make out the musty air of the damp castle. The kitchen was enormous but ultimately unimpressive. There was nothing to look at. No food obviously, a few utensils scattered about, and two large wood stoves with nothing but ash in them. But something urged me to press on, something other than curiosity. I made my way through the kitchen into the dark hallway of the servants' quarters. Even in the darkness I could make out how bleak and bland these quarters were, which by contrast made the floor above seem all the more impressive. I ascended a handsome set of stairs and entered the second floor corridor, a grand and enchanting piece of architecture, seemingly endless in both directions. The tall, arched windows stood in the orange glow of a fiery dusk as the looming August sun continued its slow dissent. Along the floor ran a tattered red carpet, which had lovely ornate bordering done in black and every hundred feet or so, there could be seen an enigmatic circular crest of the most exquisite detail. As I progressed I noticed a number of statues tucked away in little archways here and there between the corridor's myriad doors. Some of them were people, ancient, intelligent looking people holding books or strange instruments, perhaps of the scientific nature. Others depicted otherworldly avian-like creatures that stood upright like humans, hunched over with lumbering spines and grotesque beaks attached to their tiny, ill-proportioned heads. The creatures wore curious garments and had long, claw like fingers, which also held books and strange instruments. Scrolls were carved into the stonework above these statues, which held writing, perhaps a name or an inscription, but it was in a bizarre script, the characters of which I had never seen before. Though, some of the archways contained nothing but an empty stone platform, perhaps there were plans for other works of art that were never completed.

I continued on, trying various doors along the way. All were locked, but one. Its door, torn asunder from its hinges, lay at my feet. Beyond it I found an ancient library of the grandest scale. Bookshelves that stretched to the heavens lined the walls. The muted and aged greens and browns of centuries old tomes were crammed into every available nook and crevice. Horribly worn oriental rugs adorned the wooden floor in a haphazard pattern, some long ways, some slightly overlapping diagonally. The place was in the most picturesque state of disrepair one could imagine. Simple wooden tables were scattered about the library, some overturn along with the various papers and manuscripts they once held. Many of the chairs, which were of a lovely and quite curious build, reminiscent of those once found in grand opera houses, were overturned or smashed, but a few remained standing, their cushions fuzzy with mold. I came across a table with but a single book upon its surface. I opened its ancient cover as gently as one could but it immediately separated from the binding. The pages were yellow and warped with humidity. I took up a thin piece of debris from one of the destroyed chairs and used it as a blade with which to carefully turn the delicate pages without subjecting them to my fingers. It was some sort of manual for the local churches. I found a section that mentioned the Procession. There was an etching of a man holding down another man with his boot as he sawed away at his victim's neck. The inscription read, "A Parader and his offering." The book provided me with little information as many of the pages pertaining to the Procession seemed to have been crudely torn out. Most of what was left contained general information that everyone in town was well aware of-the Procession's reoccurrence every ten years, how it always falls on the full moon of the seventh lunar month, and a little bit about its ambiguous religious significance, primarily dealing with the custom of confirming the end of the Procession by the ringing of church bells, with lengthy instructions on how this custom should be carried out—the length, the timbre, the notes, etc. Of the missing pages, a decent portion of one was left behind. I could make out the first word or so of each line and all of the final line. It read:

Hail...
To thee...
Glory...
Glory...
Thy clea...
Thy gran...
Born by...
And by...
Eterna...
Glory! Glory! Glory!

Looking up from the bewildering text I noticed a small room connected to the back of the library, its entrance slightly obscured by two toppled over bookshelves. Something about it piqued my curiosity. Of course, I've always been curious about this castle, this strange and fantastic edifice that seemed to persistently linger in the back of our minds. Or perhaps it was something else. Any reasonable mind would have turned back long ago. It's true, I had no knowledge of the dangers the Castle held, but I was well aware of what lay outside its walls. So I pressed on.

I managed to climb over the shelves and make it to the narrow archway. Inside I found a curious little room with a glass-domed ceiling and decorated with a set of statues. They stood in stone boxes filled with soil, out of which ivy had at some point grown but was now yellow with death. These statues depicted women in flowing garments and the sinuous ivy, which wrapped about them, made the figures appear all the more elegant.

There were three, the left and right statues held out candles towards their respective directions while the statue in the middle stood straight, her arms reaching upwards, and her eyes fixed downward towards whoever may be looking. I stood silently for sometime, lost in the eyes of the statue as it stared down on me. The woman from my nightmares was called forth once more and the parallels made me shudder.

The sudden sound of feet and the rustle of garments broke me from the statue's mesmerizing gaze. An old set of windows sat out of place at the end of the corridor. They were fogged over and opaque with age and protected by an ornate steel grating. All that could be seen through the windows was a faint orange glow. As I walked towards them, I heard a man mumbling to himself. How in God's name can someone be living in here? I said aloud. The moment these words left my lips the strange mumbling ceased.

"Is that a patron come to visit?" Said a low and tired voice from the window. "What's your business here?" It asked. I stumbled over my speech as I attempted to explain myself. I spoke of the Procession and of the sewer, but before I could finish the voice cut in, "Ah yes, the Procession." It seemed to linger on every word. "What a lovely thing it is."

The mumbling began once more and faded away to the sound of footsteps and the rustle of garments. I stood lost in bewilderment for some time. I shouted for the strange voice to return but the vacant windows refused to speak. Suddenly, an enormous sound could be heard, as if the entire castle had shifted its weight. I followed the sound back over the toppled bookshelves and through the library to the corridor. I found its many lanterns jutting from the walls to be fully illuminated, the whole hallway bright as Christmas. It was a fantastic sight. I set out along the corridor once more. Now, illuminated by the brilliant light of the myriad lamps, I was able to better appreciate the exquisite detail of the sculptures. I came across another of the fantastic avian-like creatures and closely studied its craftsmanship. This one held an enormous scepter, at the top of which sat a lantern. The strange claws, the beak, the way its tattered garments hung from its malformed torso, truly this was the work of a once brilliant artist. I raised my hand to feel its long beak when I jumped back in fright. A twitch, a stir. I swore I had seen something. Again, there was the soft rumbling of stone. A small turn of its head. The creature broke from its pose! Its scepter began to shine a wondrous pale blue. I pressed myself against the wall in horror and awe as the creature stepped from its platform and proceeded down the corridor. Soon more rumblings could be heard, echoing through the cavernous castle. The strange creature lumbered down the corridor, his scepter shinning bright as he leaned against it with every step for support. Then I saw the others begin to leave their platforms to follow the pale blue light. The ghastly parade marched along in slow silence as night finally began to descend upon the Castle. Overcome with wonder and curiosity, or some otherworldly impulse, I followed the strange procession.

Through beautifully ornate arched-doors and up a grand stairwell, I was led to the Castle's throne room. The throne sat empty and the strange beings huddled around it as if they were waiting for someone. I stood silent in the doorway. The one with the scepter turned its head to look at me. I froze, his gaze made my feet heavy. It turned around fully and held up its scepter. The others began to manipulate their strange instruments and I quickly learned that, despite their appearance, they were not of a scientific nature. Fantastic and impossible music began to form and resound off the walls. The pale blue light beckoned me. The music soothed me. I entered the throne room. The gathering parted as I proceeded towards the throne, an ancient cathedra of unearthly material, black and gold, shinning strangely in the pale blue of the scepter. The music grew louder as I took my seat, beginning to crescendo to an ungodly level. The players formed a circle around the throne as a ghastly figure began to approach me. Tattered garments hung gracefully from its feminine form, its arms stretched out above its head, its eyes fixed downwards. It was the woman from my nightmares! She did not speak this time though. She fell to her knees and in her hand grasped an onyx-black dagger of the most bizarre and horrific design. I presented my right hand to the woman, as if I had seen this before and knew the procedure. She gently cradled my forearm as she pressed the dagger into the palm of my hand. Crimson flowed out, the skin of my palm receded into itself as the blade made its way from my wrist to the tip of my middle finger. The crowd surrounding me began to part, revealing some twisted mass that almost had a guise of humanity. It convulsed towards me, my faculties entranced by the swirling polyrhythms of the musicians. I felt myself surrender to this lurid ritual as my hand was raised so that the twisted figure may drink from my flowing wound. The room seemed to disappear around us as the being partook of my communion and the music violently vanished into silence.

A man stepped forward and began speaking a strange language I somehow understood. He said an offering has been found and that the Procession will conclude. He spoke of The Great One's chamber, gesturing towards the ceiling and I was torn from my body. Released towards the sky, my spirit crossed the zenith of the universe and I was forced to peer into the horrifying void of eternity. I was swept across ancient cosmoses and saw myself shivering, naked at the right hand of that twisted figure, which now stood upright like a man. Its tenebrous skin adorned with patches of matted black fur. Horrible appendages, that may have once been wings, jutted from its back. It held a strange instrument or weapon that seemed to be made of its own skin. We were in a barren garret atop the Castle, I convulsed amongst beds of straw and the May of lambs nuzzling at my breasts. The grotesque figure looked on with the kind of frightening approval that bespeaks an inhuman authority. A brief moment of grace fluttered across my eyelids and I violently awoke on the ancient throne, the beings staring at me. My hands were grey and misshapen. My spine felt heavy and foreign. As I opened my mouth to speak, nothing familiar could be felt and a strange language flooded from my tongue. My body floated above those fantastic beings as they watched me with excitement. The one with the scepter was banging it against the ground in horrid applause. I knew then that it had ended. I knew then why it had lasted so long. I heard the familiar church bells echoing through the city as cries of joy drowned out the last moans of death. I was taken to a little archway tucked into the wall and stood upon the platform. My new form found its natural position and I slowly fell asleep for ten years.

***

What was needed has been sought for since the last time. What was needed has been found. He rests now. The Procession has ended. The dead may finally be buried.

Hail, Great One!
To thee, we banished children call on.
To thee, our procession upon your world may cease.
Glory to He who enters the Castle!
Glory to He who gives eternal life by the Procession!
Thy cleanse our world through thy Grace.
Thy grant us life through death's release.
Born by the right hand of the Great One.
And by the light of the seventh moon.
Eternal glory bestows upon you.
Glory! Glory! Glory!

COLLECTED POEMS
Stephanie M. Wytovich

Stephanie M. Wytovich is a Professor of English by day and a horror writer by night. She is the Poetry Editor for Raw Dog Screaming Press, a book reviewer for Nameless Magazine, and a well-known coffee addict. She is a member of the Science Fiction Poetry Association, an active member of the Horror Writers Association, and a graduate of Seton Hill University's MFA program for Writing Popular Fiction. Her Bram Stoker Award-nominated poetry collections, Hysteria: A Collection of Madness, Mourning Jewelry, and An Exorcism of Angels can be found at www.rawdogscreaming.com, and her debut novel, The Eighth, will be out in 2016 from Dark Regions Press. Follow Wytovich at stephaniewytovich.blogspot.com and on twitter @JustAfterSunset.

"The Moon Makes Love to Shadows"
Setting: Cemetery

I pin my shadow to the moon and there's my silhouette
Covered in darkness and dust;
I spit the cool blackness out of my mouth
And inside my lungs grow teeth.
They swallow and purge the graveyard air inside
And laugh a wheeze that smells like dead violets.
I dance there under my mistress,
Naked and smooth as the day I was born,
My body glistening under the light of the stars
Reverberating like an echo, like a vibrating slab of flesh.
I want to kiss her
Make love to the earth below
But I am nothing but an image of the person I used to be,
I am static, a whisper

And the now moon is the only one who knows my body.

"He Writes Symphonies with My Body"
Setting: Nosferatu's Castle

There's a crackling in my head
from the silent film that's playing,
and there's a showing every night when I close my eyes,
eyes that shine like projectors,
that drip black and white,
with still frames and silent silhouettes,
with pain, with pleasure,
anticipation and fear

and yet I sit there in my bedroom,
waiting, praying, crying in mute
while shadows climb my cheekbones
and waltz into my ears
for its routine,
and I must be ready
as there's a quiet loudness in the bite of the moon, tonight
and my senses are alive with Orlock;

they're attuned to his presence and
they play a symphony of horror,
my veins as their strings—my heart as their drums—
and when he reaches for me, he holds my body like a cello,
strumming my vocal chords,
fingering my keys.

He plays me like an instrument,
and he knows where to touch,
where to blow,
and I've met no mortal man whose bite
brings immortality, whose teeth give life!
and the bruises on my neck...
they read like poetry,
circles of prose written in blacks
and in blues

So yes, I'm the climax of this concerto,
my orgasm found in between notes of blood,

but him and I—we perform in silence with quiet lust--
as we prefer to be watched
rather than heard,
viewed somewhere in between the sheets
where there is body against body,
mouth against mouth,
and no one can hear me scream.

"Ghost"
Previously published in my collection, An Exorcism of Angels
Setting: Haunted House

He called her ghost because she came and went without
Rhyme or reason and she was neither gone nor present. She
Existed as much as she knew how to, and when he'd reach out
For her, sometimes she'd let him touch her, but most of the time
All she gave him was an idea of who she really was.

"I Dream a Dream of Knives"
Setting: Haunted House/Asylum

Last night I slept with the knife in my hands,
today I woke up in the asylum. Everything is white,
but I know that I'm red, or at least that I was because I wear flowers on my wrist
blood moons on my thighs, and they must have stopped me before I gave myself a necklace, before I hugged myself to sleep, before I shot myself with the blade,
because when I choke, it's on the empty promises I made to myself,
and when I cry, it's tears of black, the curse of hysteria like tar on a woman's heart;
I laugh, but it sounds like wind chimes,
like delicate glass rubbing against each other
too afraid to make the final cut;
I scream, but it sounds like a reflection,
a rippled pool of sound in a forgotten pond,
that no hears, and no one knows how to find.

"Medicate During the Midnight Hour"
Setting: Haunted House

I fill a tea pot with Arsenic and rainwater
It's half-past storming
And I can't say your name
Can't whisper it,
Can't part my lips
And my tongue is like sandpaper
Ripping through palette
leaving crescent scars in my mouth
That taste like the blood moon
You beat me under last week
And there's a crow on my windowsill
Telling me to medicate
To do better
To feel better
To be better
But I don't like the taste of poison
Even though I take it two times a day
Even though my flesh boils in the daylight,
Though my teeth fall out at night,
So I add a lump of sugar,
Mix it with the bone from my mother's right hand,
The hand she raised to me
The fist she swung at me
And I cry
And I laugh
And I wait for the kettle, for the poison to scream,
To bleed it's feminine wail as it begins to sweat
As it begins to cry,
Begging,
Weeping,
Seeping the drips and drops of melancholy and sin

And I drink them,
Swallowing wrath and death,
Ingesting the gluttonous whore of my memories,
My damnation, my pain,
That plays, and plays, and plays
And my guilt hits hard as the poison sweeps my lungs
Whispers against my breath

Taking refuge in my liver
Making home in my heart
And in hell, mother is laughing
Cackling as I kill myself
One sip at a time,
The Devil smiling as I medicate
The crow squawking as I die.

"It was Hunger"
Previously published in my collection, Mourning Jewelry
Setting: Cemetery

And we were in love in lust and I kissed her, oh did I kiss her, and I wanted her, needed her I wrapped her legs around my neck, dove into the wet diamond of her femininity, my hair tracing circles on her milk white thighs as I left crimson kisses on her flesh, it was sublime, it was ecstasy and I was cutting and tearing, biting listening to her scream, and she came in waves of blood and I drank it up like the wine it was, cherry red and sweet as I ate her from the outside in.

"Two of Swords"
Setting: Haunted House

It's still suffocating
These memories,
These images in my head—
I cut the deck,
Swallow my pride.
My cards are sharp
With crying towers
and lovers that have never seen hearts.
There's smoke coming from the eyes
Of the woman holding two blades crisscrossed against her chest,
Her neck slit in invisible haste as conflict broods
In her taut, stitched lips.
I sigh.
My throat swells from words I cannot speak.

Why does the moon hate the way I breathe?
The universe despise the way I love?

I touch the cards, a Vitruvian spread
That spits fire at my future,
Weaving madness,
Spilling blood,
And my stars align in Hell,
While Aries, my ram,
Runs into the same wall
Over and over and over again;
A stubborn beast who
Makes the same mistakes,
Cries the same tears,
Kills the same dreams,
And I sit there and watch,
A bystander to what fate has foretold,
A destiny written in storms,
Forged in spilled ink and lost treasures,
And I am the mistress to all things forgotten
Things that were
And things that never shall be.

"When I Birthed a Monster, I Birthed Myself"
Setting: Cemetery

None of this feels real; my being is a crafted illusion,
a nightmare that I walk through, that I wake up in,
that I've learned to cope with while I've stayed buried in the shadows,
while I've stayed hidden in plain sight. This entity that's inside of me,
this death, this human rot,
it allows me to sense everything and nothing,
a reversed sociopath who feels too much instead of too little,
and the darkness in my eyes makes me a monster, a monster with
dandelions in her heart and sorrow braided into her hair. My daily routine
is a drink of poison, a non-stop ache in my chest, and I vomit the version
of myself that I hate as I cry over the girl I wish I was—the girl I used to
be—
the girl I lost all those years ago on country roads, in liquor bottles,
in punctured organs and well-composed lies. I made myself a monster
because
the human version of me wasn't strong enough. She cried and broke one
too many times,
and she tried, but she died, died one too many deaths, and this version is
what
resurrected, what had to be born, what had to be made,
and if you look close enough in my eyes, you can see the blood of the
woman I used to be,
she's still there, bleeding, trying to survive.

"Winter Canvas"
Inspired by Michael Marshall Smith's piece "Curving Path"
Previously published on his website
Setting: Cemetery

Winter is a dust-covered palette,
a cumulus memory
in diluted ink;
it survives in blacks and grays,
in crows and fresh ash,
and I paint a forest of trees as barren as I am,
their branches like arthritic arms
holding me against the wind
but it hurts and
I cough on icicles,
see my breath on its canvas,
an impasto of sickness and age;
I use its solstice brush to smear
charcoal against the sky,
a chiaroscuro background of
feathers and soot
yet while blended and blurred,
a path evolves towards spring
and I curve it out of darkness,
make it bone,
virginal in asylum-white,
but this blank madness is a snow bank,
a chest of clouds that hold the secret to rebirth
to second chances,
but it's too bright for my sorrow
so I cover it, too, in shadows
of storm,
in a thunderous moor
uncontained by page
by season
or by art,
and now I can sleep,
sleep sound and sleep tight,
hibernate with snowflakes
that kiss my hair like serpents,
curl up with the wind that
screams my dreams

into nightmares.

"What it Takes to Sing the Blues"
Setting: Castle Ball

There's a canary in my ribcage
and she's dying, rattling against
my ivory bars with her death songs
and her high-pitched wails. I want to
reach inside and strangle her—finish
the job for the winged beast
I swallowed for my career,
but there's something about the
tone of her death that gives my voice a rasp,
a touch of melancholy that brings audience's to tears, and all it takes
is my lying down on the piano so she suffocates, wheezes, and hacks,
and then, and only then, can I properly sing the blues.

"Bathory"
Previously published in my collection, Hysteria: A Collection of Madness
Setting: Bathory's Castle

Her hair cascaded
Down her back
In a flight of ravens
Against milk-white flesh
Bloodied from her
Midnight suitor

Drained of her age
She bathed in virginity
Rubbing it into
Her skin to moisturize
The wear on her body
Collected from centuries past

Her fingernails
Cut like knives
As she opened their chests
Shearing them like wool
So she could steal their years
To regain her youth

She drank their juices,
Savoring the crimson elixirs
Each its own brand
Like a fresh, summer wine
Ripened in its adolescence
Begging to breathe

Her children sang
Songs of death
 Butchered at the hands
Of unattainable vanity
Courtesy of the Hungarian devil
Erzsebet, the countess of blood

"Monster, Me"
Previously published in my collection, An Exorcism of Angels
Previously featured in HWA Poetry Showcase, Vol. 1
Setting: Cemetery

Inside of me, there's a sickness. A darkness that breeds and snuffs out
the good, filling me with screams and cobwebs and an emptiness
that infects everything that was once alive. It's a slow death and I feel
everything: every touch, every kiss, every parting. Sometimes I even think
my heart
stops beating; it just quiets and goes kind of still, barely working until it's
not. I know it's her, and I know she holds me tighter than any lover I've
ever known, and I hate her—but oh do I love her—and no matter how
hard I try to fight, how desperately I try not to give in, she's always there,
waiting, ready, and willing to take me as I am. Broken. Tired. Weak. She
loves and accepts the tragedy of my being and she understands the cuts and
the bruises, the stitches
and the scars.

I call her monster and she moves within me, finding her comfort spot
where she nestles down deep until her arms are mine, until my legs
are hers. I see through two pairs of eyes, and breathe with four lungs, and
the disease
that breeds in my stomach is not a cancer of the flesh, but a mutation of the
heart. She's
the cure to my epidemic, my anti-suicide machine, and together we/I walk
through this life, holding hands and hearts, whispering secrets and drinking
down poisons, mixing black magic
remedies and sucking down sage, and together we/I live, somehow we/I
survive. My monster, me. The Jekyll to my Hyde